You'll never get enough of these cowboys!

Talented Harlequin Blaze author
Debbie Rawlins keeps the cowboys
coming with her popular miniseries

Made in Montana

The little town of Blackfoot Falls
isn't so sleepy anymore....
In fact, it seems everyone's staying up late!

Get your hands on a hot cowboy with

#789 *Alone with You*
(March 2014)

#801 *Need You Now*
(June 2014)

#812 *Behind Closed Doors*
(September 2014)

*And remember,
the sexiest cowboys are Made in Montana!*

Dear Reader,

Welcome back to the world of Made in Montana! I think you'll find this book a little different from the others. It's a love story that takes place over the course of a road trip. Lexy Worthington's job depends on getting stubborn-as-a-mule, sexy rodeo champion Will Tanner all the way from Montana to Houston, Texas, in time for a photo shoot he is dead set against.

First, he refuses to fly, then he insists on driving his old trailer (called Betsy) or the deal's off. Short on cash, trust and patience, Lexy has no choice but to travel with him. If she can make it to Houston without strangling him, her future will be safe and secure, and if she never sees Tanner again, it'll be too soon.

I confess, I totally fell in love with Tanner when he watched a young rodeo cowboy tweet his scores to fans. Tanner, a little wiser, and much older, realizes it might be time to hang up his spurs in this crazy new rodeo world of young bucks shunning beer for vitamin drinks and worrying about how to market themselves. What he ought to do is rest his weary bones and make himself a T-shirt that says "Real Men Don't Tweet." Poor Tanner, but lucky Lexy (and me), because he stole my heart at that moment, and steering him toward his happy ending was more fun than I can say.

I hope you enjoy the ride!

Love,

Debbi

Alone with You

—

Debbi Rawlins

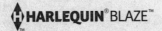

Recycling programs
for this product may
not exist in your area.

ISBN-13: 978-0-373-79793-6

ALONE WITH YOU

Copyright © 2014 by Debbi Quattrone

Printed in U.S.A.

ABOUT THE AUTHOR

Debbi Rawlins grew up in the country with no fast-food drive-throughs or nearby neighbors, so one might think as a kid she'd be dazzled by the bright lights of the city, the allure of the unfamiliar. Not so. She loved Westerns in movies and books, and her first crush was on a cowboy—okay, he was an actor in the role of a cowboy, but she was only eleven, so it counts. It was in Houston, Texas, where she first started writing for Harlequin, and now, more than fifty books later, she has her own ranch...of sorts. Instead of horses, she has four dogs, five cats, a trio of goats and free-range cattle keeping her on her toes on a few acres in gorgeous rural Utah. And of course, the deer and elk are always welcome.

Books by Debbi Rawlins

To get the inside scoop on Harlequin Blaze and its talented writers, be sure to check out blazeauthors.com.

For Jolie and Jill, my plotting posse,
who listen to me whine
and know when to bring out the whip.

1

THE LAST THING Alexis Worthington wanted to do was beg for a job. Especially from her own father. She watched the numbers climb on the elevator as she rode to the top floor of the family's downtown Oklahoma City building. Then she went straight to the ladies' room to check that her updo was still tucked in and her conservative blue suit was lint free, and most important to meet with Norma, her father's longtime assistant. She pushed open the door and relaxed for the first time that morning.

"Oh, my goodness, Alexis, look at you." Norma, her auburn hair swept into the same French twist she'd worn since the nineties, shook her head fondly. "You're looking more and more like your mother."

"And you look younger than when I saw you last year. How does that work?" Lexy's laugh broke into a cough when Norma nearly squeezed the breath out of her.

The woman stood barely five feet but she had strong, wiry arms and a steel will to match. She was the perfect assistant for Marshall Worthington and had stuck it out with him for over twenty years. Lexy only wished her own mother was as capable of going toe-to-toe with him.

Norma moved back to hold Lexy at arm's length. "Why are you dressed like a funeral director?"

"Gee, thanks." Lexy quickly smoothed back the tendril of hair Norma had dislodged. "This is an Armani suit and I think I look very professional."

Norma sighed. "You do. You just don't look like you."

"Today isn't about me," she said quietly. This was about getting back in her father's good graces. Eight years and he still hadn't forgiven her for not going to Harvard.

"You have a point. He's awfully stubborn."

Stubborn wasn't the word Lexy would have gone for. Infuriating. Ultraconservative. Controlling. But that wasn't all he was, and she couldn't afford to forget that he'd been a loving father. Until she'd chosen her own path.

God, she hated having to grovel. Hated it.

No, she refused to look at it that way. All she'd ever wanted was to join the family business and she'd prepared herself by learning the workings of the The Worthington Group inside and out. Besides, she was qualified and her father knew it.

She faced herself in the mirror and plucked a tiny piece of lint off the wool blazer. The damn suit had cost her a fortune. She wouldn't have minded the expense if it hadn't pushed her dangerously close to maxing out her last credit card. But she needed to appear confident, successful, even though Marshall Worthington would see right through her. It wouldn't matter. Appearances meant everything to her father.

"We should go," Norma said, squeezing Lexy's hand before leading the way.

Together, they walked past a pretty, fresh-faced blonde manning the reception desk. "Remember the summer I spent sitting right there?" It had been the month between junior and senior year of prep school. She'd gone to the house in St. Thomas for part of her break. But she'd quickly grown bored and thought it would be useful to get to know more about the company.

"Of course I remember. Marshall couldn't have been more pleased."

Back then it seemed Lexy could do no wrong. Full of promise, competitive to a fault, she'd been Daddy's little girl. The golden child. Until everything had gone to hell. "What's with all the art deco?" The lobby had been the very picture of tradition, and now it was gleaming with chrome and lacquer.

"Harrison," Norma said.

"Wow. I'll give it to him. He must have been very convincing to win Dad over." Lexy tried to not feel resentful. Bitterness would only derail her meeting. Besides, she had no right. She sure hadn't given her brother's feelings a thought when the attention and praise were centered on her. She'd been far too selfish, her sense of entitlement off the charts. Easy to see now, so at least she could be grateful for losing the blinders. Besides, she wasn't looking to replace Harrison. She only wanted him to scoot over a little.

They'd reached her father's office, his huge double doors still the same sturdy oak. She paused a moment, wondering if recanting would've been enough for him. Had she backed down and gone to Harvard like he wanted, would her life have turned out differently? Or would he have held it against her for daring to have her own opinion?

Sadly, her decision to go to Stanford had had nothing to do with sound reasoning and everything to do with Hunter Livingston. After dating him for six months they'd agreed to apply to Stanford together. It had never occurred to her that her father would object. And with such vehemence. Before she knew it, her innocent act of independence had escalated to full-blown rebellion.

Ironically, her relationship with Hunter hadn't made it to freshman year. But the war with her father had quietly raged on.

"I assume he's in there."

"Yes. So is Harrison."

"Are they just finishing up?" she asked, hoping she'd be meeting her father alone.

"No, I'm afraid your brother fully intends to stick his nose where it doesn't belong."

Lexy sighed. "So they're waiting for me."

Norma nodded. "It's shameful, their treating this like an interview. You have as much right to help run this company as Harrison does. I haven't spoken to your father for two days." She slipped behind her desk, tugged down the hem of her black blazer and lowered her voice. "I don't even know if the idiot noticed."

That made Lexy smile.

Norma pressed the intercom buzzer with a manicured red nail, announced Lexy's arrival, then released the button before her father could respond. Wonderful. That must've improved his mood.

"Don't take any guff from them, you hear me?" Norma's warning frown eased. "It's good to have you back."

Switching her purse to her left hand, Lexy murmured, "Let's not get ahead of ourselves."

Norma's expression fell. "That doesn't sound like the girl I know."

That headstrong idealist hadn't been up to her eyeballs in debt. Still, the sadness in Norma's green eyes got to Lexy and she pulled back her shoulders. "You're right. I'm going to totally kill this," she said, and smiled at the alarm in the older woman's face. "It's slang. And it's a good thing."

"Oh. Well, then, go kill it."

Lexy paused, her hand on the doorknob. Maybe Harrison was sticking around to give her moral support. He was actually a pretty good brother most of the time. Okay, *some* of the time.

She found a smile the second before she opened the door.

"Good morning, Father," she said, not surprised to see him sitting behind his antique mahogany desk.

He nodded. "Good morning, Alexis. You're right on time."

When she didn't immediately see Harrison, she thought Norma might've been mistaken. And then Lexy spotted him, sitting on the couch against the back wall, directly under the Monet. His relaxed posture couldn't hide the frost in his eyes.

"Hello, Harrison, good to see you." She tensed when he didn't respond. So what…he felt threatened? Too bad. There was plenty of room in the company for both of them.

It would serve Harrison right if she sat with her back to him but they weren't kids anymore. She settled in a chair that mostly faced her father without her position being rude to her brother. "The lobby looks great," she said. "Nice, clean lines but still warm and inviting."

"I'm still getting used to all that chrome," Marshall said with just enough disdain to get his disapproval across. "I've promised to give it another month."

"I'm glad you like it." Harrison moved to sit closer to Lexy. "We're branching out into new arenas. I feel it's appropriate for the company to have a fresh face. Show we're in step with the times, that we're as relevant now as we were three generations back."

"Good taste never goes out of style," her father said, his censoring gaze switching from Harrison to Lexy.

Oh, yeah, this was starting out well. Both of them looking for her to be an ally.

"Tell me about the new directions you're exploring," she said, and saw a hint of a smile lift the corners of her father's mouth. He must have liked the way she'd taken control of the conversation.

Harrison started in, suddenly brimming with enthusiasm. Until he was cut off with a raised hand.

"Let's not get ahead of ourselves." Marshall's frown emphasized the lines creasing his forehead and fanning out at the corners of his blue eyes. "I hope you have your résumé with you. And your transcripts. I'd like to see what kind of education Stanford provided."

Her temper flared. She'd known this wouldn't be easy but she'd hoped he wouldn't be petty. "Really, Dad? You don't know where I've been working or what I've been doing for the past three years?" Her annoyance was met with silence. "Either way, does it matter?"

He studied her for a moment, then hit his intercom button. "Norma, would you please send in coffee?"

Lexy dug into her briefcase as she took a couple of calming breaths. "Here," she said, leaning forward to slide the papers across his desk. "My résumé and transcripts."

She saw the ghost of a smile again and knew he was impressed that she'd stayed a step ahead of him.

At least now, for the most part, she could read him. As a child she'd been incapable of deciphering the peculiar mix of respect and frustration he seemed to feel for her. He admired her independence and strong will right up until she defied something he held sacrosanct.

From as far back as she could remember, relatives, employees—everyone—had commented on how much she was like her father. They were both smart, goal-oriented and driven.

But that's where the similarities ended. Her father was dogmatic in the single-mindedness that propelled him through life. While she cared about the company, a lot more than her father or anyone else realized, there was more to her than the Worthington name. Yes, she'd do almost anything to protect their image, but she had her own line in the sand.

"I see you've had only one long-term job since graduate school," he said, scanning the first page. "Why is that?"

"I wondered that myself after I'd interviewed nonstop for several months. I finally figured out it had to do with my last name."

He looked up. "I hope you aren't implying I interfered."

"Not at all." She smiled. "You didn't have to."

He held her gaze for a long disconcerting moment. If he cut the meeting short it would be her fault. Dammit, she'd promised herself she wouldn't bait him. She needed this job more than she needed to be right.

After a brief knock, the door opened. Norma rolled in a coffee service, which she pushed toward the sofas and conference table.

"Not there," Harrison said. "Here will be fine. We shouldn't be much longer."

Norma blinked, then looked to Marshall for confirmation.

Lexy had no idea if he'd responded nonverbally. Her gaze had gone from Norma to her brother. When their eyes met, the contempt that swept his features startled her. Why was he running hot and cold? She hadn't done anything to him. Harrison had always been the yes-sir, no-sir type, waiting to express his scorn behind their father's back. He'd applauded her defiance. Called her his hero.

"You still take your coffee black, honey?" Norma laid a hand on her shoulder.

Lexy looked up and smiled. "I wouldn't turn down a squirt of agave if you have it."

"Just so happens we do."

Harrison gave Norma a stern look, which she ignored by pouring from the sterling-silver coffeepot that had been in the family for years.

"Since when do we have agave?" he asked, emphasizing the word as if it were a curse.

"Since I bought it, dear," Norma said sweetly.

Lexy stifled a laugh. Harrison was clearly trying to

make some sort of point, probably that Norma had gone out of her way for Lexy. But he was no match for the stalwart Norma, and he should've learned that lesson by now.

She passed out the filled china cups, and only then did Lexy dare to look up. And saw that her father also was holding back a smile. Their gazes met, briefly, and warmth filled Lexy's chest. For one crazy moment she was Daddy's little girl again, the two of them sharing a private joke.

"So...you were telling us why you haven't been able to hold down a job," Harrison said.

Lexy shot him an I'll-be-damned-if-I'll-answer-to-you look, which promptly shut him up. It had never mattered that he was older. She'd been stronger, more outspoken, and he'd rarely challenged her. Maybe that was the reason he felt threatened by her return. "Thank you, Norma," she said, taking her first sip. "This is perfect."

"Let me know if you need anything else." She addressed Lexy, ignoring the two men, then pushed the cart to the side and left the office.

Her father's attention returned to the résumé, his eyes giving nothing away when he finally glanced up. "An account exec? You must've been bored."

"Yes, as a matter of fact." Her own fault. That's what he was thinking, and he wasn't wrong.

"So what brings you back now?" He leaned back in his black leather chair and regarded her over steepled fingers.

"I've always wanted to work for the company. But you already know that."

He smiled a little. "I thought perhaps you'd decided otherwise. After all, your call came out of the blue."

"I was let go from Mattheson and Myers." She leaned forward to set down her coffee. Knowing better than to risk marking the mahogany, she thought it fitting to leave the cup and saucer on her Stanford transcripts. It still rankled that he'd asked for them. "The company signed a new client who they believed would consider my employment a conflict of interest."

"Ah. A former customer of ours, I presume?"

"I don't know. They kept the name confidential."

Harrison snorted. "So we're the consolation prize?"

Lexy swiveled around to look him directly in the eye. "Is that what you think?"

"Don't turn this back on me." His face reddened. "I worked here every summer during college and grad school, then started full-time the day after I got my Harvard degree. And I've busted my ass for this company every day since."

She knew he'd throw in Harvard. "You can work hard or you can work smart. I didn't make that choice for you." They'd engaged in a mild rivalry at prep school. She'd had the better grades, while he'd always studied much harder. She pressed her lips together before taking a deep breath. "Look, Harrison, I know you've earned your place here. I'm simply looking for the chance to earn mine."

He blinked, then looked away.

Lexy knew her father was watching them. He'd encouraged their competitiveness as children. She hoped he didn't still consider it a good idea. Ignoring him, she addressed her brother. "You mentioned branching out in other areas. Tell me about it."

Harrison sipped his coffee, his brow furrowed, clearly torn over whether to trust her or not. The realization made her sad.

Finally, he cleared his throat, made eye contact again. "Sports. Equipment, outdoor gear, that sort of thing, but also team ownership. The consumer's consciousness has been raised to return to American products. I'm sure you're aware that we took several hits from the media over sending jobs abroad." He shrugged as if his solution was a no-brainer. "What's more American than baseball or football?"

She wasn't sure what to say. This was quite a departure

from their grassroots business of brand foods and paper products, and eventually, real estate. Not just that, but she didn't understand how owning a sports team made the company more patriotic.

"Alexis, you look surprised."

She turned to her father while she searched for the right words. The last thing she wanted to do was second-guess Harrison. "Frankly, I am. But it's an interesting concept. I'd like to hear more."

Her father's laugh was brief and without humor. "You want to earn a place at The Worthington Group, then speak your mind. God knows you've never had any trouble before."

He was right, and while she could grovel a bit, she wasn't about to change who she was. "The public isn't wrong. We should be keeping more jobs at home. Providing American jobs was part of the foundation this company was built on. That being said, I'm not clear yet as to how sports will complement the company's brand."

She didn't bother to look at her brother. Tension radiated from him and she didn't doubt he placed the blame for this farce at her feet. Then again, she could've blindly endorsed his plans in a show of solidarity. But that wasn't in her nature. She liked to know the facts. Explore every angle. Make sure she was in control before facing off with Marshall Worthington.

"Tell you what," he said, pushing her résumé toward her. "I'll give you a chance to see for yourself. Harrison has someone working on a campaign for a men's fragrance line that's positioned to tie in to the sports theme. What is it—" he glanced at Harrison "—a cowboy calendar that women are supposed to vote on?"

"A calendar." Lexy sighed. She couldn't help it. Yes, the idea of a beefcake calendar made her want to gag, but equally revolting was her father's lack of pretense. He was determined to drag her through the mud before giving her a serious position.

"That's Karina's project," Harrison said, his voice tight and angry. "She doesn't need any help."

"Isn't the photo shoot scheduled for next week?"

"Yes."

"It's my understanding that she has yet to sign the final candidate."

Harrison frowned. He was probably thinking the same thing as Lexy. Why would their father even know something so trivial? "You did set stringent parameters." Harrison set his cup and saucer down clumsily. "The top-seed rodeo stars aren't convinced that endorsing a fragrance is a smart move. Yet."

That in itself should've given Harrison his first clue, Lexy thought, but kept silent.

"I made it clear. We play in the big leagues or we don't play at all." Her father's chilly gaze bore into Harrison's.

Lexy's eyes were the same color blue but she fervently hoped they never looked that cold and hard. "I still don't understand what you want from me," she said, even though she had the horrific feeling she knew exactly what he intended.

"You've always been quick on your feet, Alexis. And quite persuasive. A week should be sufficient for you to find an acceptable candidate so we can finally put this—" he waved dismissively "—business to rest."

"You never intended to let me see this project through." Harrison stood, flushed with anger. "Did you?"

Annoyance flashed across their father's face. "Have you ever known me to vacillate? You asked, I said yes. The ball's in your court. I'm even offering your sister to help you."

"And if I don't want her help?"

He leaned back, an amused gleam in his eyes. "Then

perhaps I should give her your office and leave you free to run all the fool's errands you want."

Lexy stared down at her clasped hands. Could this meeting be any more dreadful? She couldn't look at Harrison, even though she felt awful for him. Their father had always been a stern taskmaster, but he hadn't been cruel.

Harrison had played the dutiful son, attended Harvard, resisted his odd penchant for women who many would consider tacky and inappropriate. After school he'd taken no time to blow off steam but immediately joined the company. He didn't deserve this treatment.

Knowing this, she still said nothing in his defense. She simply allowed the silence to fester. Until Harrison left the office without another word. Only then did she look up. "Was that really necessary?"

"Don't tell me you're getting soft."

That line in the sand? She could feel her toes right up against it. God, she really should tell him to keep his job, that she no longer wanted it. But she couldn't face the growing list of creditors. "Fine. What's next?" she asked, lifting her chin.

"Go to Human Resources and fill out the necessary paperwork. Then I suggest you get out there and find the right cowboy."

Lexy didn't say another word as she rose and let herself out. Human Resources? Really? For God's sake.

Norma was waiting for her. "I knew he'd pull something like this," she said, and waved a hand when Lexy smiled. "Of course I was listening. I had a feeling he was up to no good and I wanted to be prepared. Right after you called last week he asked me to check on the status of the calendar…which we both know he doesn't give a tinker's damn about." She slipped around her desk. "When I told him they were having trouble finding the last man, he seemed mighty pleased. So I asked myself, what is the old goat up to?"

Lexy watched her pull a manila folder from her bottom drawer and then motion for Lexy to follow. They walked quickly to the elevators and got into the first private car.

"This man's endorsement contract with us expires in just under two weeks," Norma said, holding up the folder. "Harrison signed him for that ridiculous Sundowner accessory line that failed. But the guy is perfect. He's a bareback bronc rider who's won two world championships, gold buckles, million-dollar purses, the whole thing. I remembered him because my Henry is such a big rodeo fan. This Tanner fellow is over thirty and on the downslide right now so maybe he'll do it." Norma passed her the folder. "Worth a try."

"Why didn't you give this to the woman who's in charge of the project?"

"Frankly, I'd hoped I was wrong and your father wouldn't send you on a wild-goose chase just to show you who's boss. It pains me to see him treat you this way." She squeezed Lexy's hand. "If it had turned out I'd misread Marshall, I would've given Harrison the file. But Karina?" Norma sniffed. "I do not care for that woman."

Lexy grinned. "Norma, you're the absolute best." The elevator doors slid open and Lexy stuffed the folder into her purse. If her father expected failure, she couldn't wait to disappoint him.

2

Leaning on a cedar post and watching the last saddle bronc event, Will Tanner muttered a curse when he saw his friend go flying over the mare's head. Charlie hit the ground, landing hard on his ass, but jumped up quick as a jackrabbit. The crowd roared from the stands, surging to their feet with applause when Charlie whipped off his hat and waved it. He'd been around the circuit for a long time and was a fan favorite, even when he was losing. Something that happened too often lately. Just like with Tanner.

"That ol' guy sure can take a lotta punishment." Clay stood next to him, one foot propped on the bottom rail. He reached in his jeans' pocket, glanced at his fancy iPhone, then looked at Tanner. "You been busted up pretty good in your day. How many bones have you broken?"

In your day.

The words were as irritating as a yipping coyote.

Tanner squinted at the fresh-faced kid who was barely twenty. Probably only started shaving last year. Didn't stop him from trying to grow one of those dumb little soul patches. "Enough," Tanner said, turning back to see Charlie limp to the gate, watching for the scores to go up.

He was only thirty-four, a year older than Tanner, and had the good sense to announce that after this year he was done rodeoing. It was gonna be strange following the tour without Charlie. For over twelve years, even when they hadn't traveled or bunked together, their paths had regularly crossed. But that's the way it was with most of the veteran riders. They'd all played poker together, got drunk together and chased women. Until they started winning gold buckles and didn't have to do the chasing anymore.

Clay's thumbs worked feverishly on the cell's keypad. Tanner still hadn't gotten the hang of texting. Hell, half the time he couldn't remember to turn on his relic of a phone. When he did, it usually needed charging.

"So where you headed next?" Clay asked, his attention focused on the small screen until he finished his message and stuffed the iPhone back in his pocket. He caught Tanner's frown. "I was just tweeting my scores."

Tanner nodded like he understood. This new breed of cowboy was something else. They drank protein shakes instead of beer, fretted over their exercise regimens and sat around discussing their marketability.

Damn, he was gonna miss Charlie. The two of them had both come from flyspeck towns and started young, before iPhones and Facebook and Twitter took over the world. Maybe they should retire together and make T-shirts and bumper stickers that read Real Men Don't Tweet.

"Where did you say you're going?" Clay asked again.

"New Mexico." Tanner backed away from the railing, adjusting his Stetson and peering up at the clear Montana sky. He had a few hours before nightfall. Enough time to get on the road and find a place to park his trailer overnight. No sense sticking around. His scores couldn't carry him to the next round. "You?"

"I'm riding in Wyoming in two weeks. My sister's got a ranch in Colorado. I might hang out there in the meantime." Clay jerked a look somewhere over Tanner's shoulder. "Unless I get a better offer." Before he could turn and see what had put the cocky grin on Clay's face, the kid said, "Look sharp, old man. I believe that lady's trying to get your attention."

Tanner swung toward the parking lot in time to see a leggy blonde in skin-tight jeans wave. He smiled and waved back. Maybe he wouldn't be so quick to leave tonight.

"No, not Ariel," Clay said, unwrapping a stick of gum. "She's waiting for me. The other one."

"Where?" Unlike his stiff back and shoulders, his vision was just fine and he couldn't see another living soul.

"Ariel's kind of blocking her, but she's behind the fence to the right."

Tanner squinted and saw part of a female outline fading into the dark SUV behind her. She was on the short side, brown hair, pulled back, sunglasses taking up half her face and dressed kind of stodgy in a navy blue blazer and matching slacks. "What makes you think she's waiting for me?"

"I figured she was looking to interview you for that AARP magazine." Clay laughed.

Tanner knocked off the smart ass's hat, then chuckled when Clay had to scramble to catch the Stetson before it blew too far. "It ain't right you trying to make a man feel over the hill at thirty-three. You just wait…your time will come, kid. Sooner than you think." At least it had for Tanner. If he stuck it out for two more years, half his life officially would've been spent rodeoing.

He had no regrets. Even if he'd had the money for college he wouldn't have gone. His younger brother was the one with a head for learning, and he was glad he'd been able to send him to a good university. Doug had even gone on to law school, courtesy of Tanner's winnings. He considered the money well spent.

"Why the hell did you have to do that in front of Ariel?" Clay brushed off the hat and set it back on his head.

Tanner slid another look at the blonde, her teeth gleaming an unnatural white. The shorter brunette had moved closer but the high chain-link fence prevented her from approaching. Other women had gathered near the exit, most of them buckle bunnies, but also a few moms trying to get autographs for their youngsters.

This was the part he dreaded lately. Signing autographs wasn't a big deal. He'd never minded, especially when it was for kids, but it felt a lot better to scrawl his name when he was scoring high and taking home prize money. At other times it was a mob scene and all he wanted was to get to his trailer and let a hot shower pelt his aching body.

Today wasn't bad. His shoulder hurt less than it had all week. Meaning he wouldn't mind some feminine company. The redhead standing by herself caught his eye. She was just his type. Tall, lean, not too skimpy in the chest department, and he didn't give one damn that her fancy Charlie 1 Horse hat and satin-trimmed Western shirt were just for show. He was gonna like her a whole lot more without them on.

"I'm taking off," he said, keeping an eye on the redhead. He wanted to get to her before one of the other guys did.

"You're not waiting for Charlie or Bryce?"

"Nah, they're both headed for Texas." Something Tanner had thought about doing. His grandparents lived in Texas but he'd seen them last month when he'd done some repairs around the ranch while enjoying Nana's home cooking. He made a point of seeing her and Pop regularly. They were more like parents to him and Doug, taking them in after their mother had been killed. They hadn't even asked for a penny of child support from his old man. Probably knew the bum wouldn't have coughed up anything, anyhow. "See ya around, kid."

"Yeah, sure." Clay shot a look toward the fence. "Don't even think about stealing Ariel," he said with a faint grin that didn't hide his worried expression.

"She's too young for me." Tanner clapped him on the back. "Anyway, I don't poach."

"Yeah, I know you don't. Not like some of those other guys who have gold buckles."

Tanner smiled, then strolled toward the exit. He knew who Clay meant but no way would he get into a conversation about it. None of his business. He kept to himself when it came to matters of politics, religion and sex. And Betsy. Anyone who knew him the tiniest bit knew better than to disrespect his fifth wheel. A lot of the guys drove around in fancy buses equipped with everything from satellite dishes to hot tubs. Some even had hired men or relatives to drive them around. Not him. He and poor rattling Betsy had been together for ten years now. And he had every intention of driving her to his last rodeo.

He slipped through the gate and got close enough to see that the redhead had a real nice smile and sexy green eyes that warned him he'd have to watch himself. Though he'd like to think he was too old and wise to do anything stupid, he'd been thrown off guard a time or two by a green-eyed female.

Before he reached her, two boys and their mom bushwhacked him. Nodding politely, he asked their names, and signed his across the bottom of a magazine picture taken of him at the San Antonio Stock Show. He'd always appreciated the fans, but nowadays, he prized their loyalty all the more. He let the boys inspect his buckle and answered a question about where he kept the gold ones while he slyly scoped out the redhead.

God bless her, that smile was aimed right at him. He smiled back and tipped the rim of his Stetson. She tossed her long hair. Always a good sign.

The boys were herded off by their mom but before he could move, three more kids cornered him. He got them squared away by answering more questions and signing their ball caps. He hoped no one else wanted anything because the redhead was starting to look impatient.

"Mr. Tanner?"

The voice came from behind. No one called him that. Just Tanner. He stopped and turned. It was the woman Clay had pointed out earlier. She looked overheated in the blue suit. Her face was flushed and her cheeks damp. She held a hand up to shade her eyes from the broiling afternoon sun, though he figured the big, dark glasses would've done the job.

"What can I do for you?"

"I'm Alexis Worthington," she said, extending her hand. "From The Worthington Group."

"Okay." If that was supposed to mean something to him it missed the mark. He pulled off his glove. Her hand was small and soft.

"I called you earlier and left a message."

He automatically touched his shirt pocket where his phone would've been had he remembered to bring it. "I haven't turned my phone on yet today."

Her arched brows rose above her glasses as if he'd committed a sin. "Actually, I left you a message last night, as well."

"Don't know why I didn't get that one. I wasn't drunk." He glanced at the redhead and saw that she was distracted by someone or something in the direction of the arena. "Look, ma'am, I'm kind of in the middle of something," he said and started walking again, hoping to catch the redhead's eye.

The short brunette stayed with him. "I understand. When will you be free?"

"For what?"

"To talk." She checked her wristwatch. "Let's set a time."

He got the other woman's attention again, and smiling, she leaned a hip against a sleek silver convertible. Tanner hoped the car belonged to her. He wouldn't mind a ride in that honey. She pushed off and straightened when he reached her, the tip of her tongue slipping out to moisten her glossy pink lips. Man, she was tall. At a good six feet, he didn't beat her by much.

"You waiting for anyone in particular, darlin'?" He smiled, removed his hat and finger-combed his hair.

"Mr. Tanner."

Red blinked, then frowned down at the shorter woman still nipping at his heels.

"What?" he growled. Hell, he thought he'd lost her.

"I'm trying to arrange a time for us to talk."

"Lady, I don't even know who you are. And you gotta stop calling me *Mr.* Tanner." His father was still a fixture around the tour, and Tanner had the misfortune of running into him on occasion.

"Then I presume you go by Will?"

"No. Tanner. Just Tanner."

The redhead let out a soft, delicate snort, and they both looked at her. Her lips started to form a pout. Much as he wasn't fond of pouters, she had a fetching mouth.

He smiled, moved a little closer. "Would you excuse me for ten seconds, darlin'? I promise, just ten."

"All right," she drawled, sighing, and getting him excited when she leaned into him, her warm, sweet breath drifting along the side of his neck. "I'm Kimberly."

"That's a pretty name." He fixed his gaze on the tiny dimple at the corner of her mouth.

"Hey." The brunette pest touched his arm. "How about six?"

Dammit, she was like an irritating gnat you couldn't get rid of. And she was crazy. "Tonight?"

"Yes." She removed her dark glasses and squinted at her fancy gold watch. "That's in two hours. Plenty of time to…" Her voice trailed off as she abruptly brought her chin up and turned to stare at Kimberly. "That line worked? You just met him and you're going to— Look, I'm not judging. I'm curious." Just as abruptly, she turned back to him, tilting her head and looking him up and down as if he were on the auction block. "Hmm, maybe this will work, after all."

"I'm sorry," he said to Kimberly. The blush staining her cheeks worried him. So did the way she jerked back when he touched her wrist. "I don't know this whack job. We'll ignore her and—"

Kimberly inhaled sharply. "Maybe another time." She backed away, rounding the rear of the convertible and hurrying toward the arena gate.

"Nice." Disgusted, Tanner stuck the Stetson back on his head as he watched the redhead of his dreams make tracks. "Thanks. Good job." He turned to the brunette, hoping she'd embarrassed herself.

She was checking out his ass. "Clean you up a bit and this could work," she murmured, then lifted her gaze and stared at him with eyes as clear and blue as the summer sky. "What?" she asked. "Her?" She cocked her head in the direction of the arena. "Oh, please, you can get laid anytime."

He snorted. "From your lips to God's ears." He watched her dig inside a purse big enough to be a briefcase, then pull out a folder. "Who did you say you were?"

"Alexis Worthington."

"Am I supposed to know you?"

"No, but you should be familiar with the company for which I work."

For which I work. She was one of *those*. "And which company would that be?" This woman wasn't from one of his sponsors. He only had two left and he knew their reps. He glanced down at her dusty conservative shoes, then swung a longing look after the redhead. But she'd already disappeared.

"The Worthington Group," she said as if it was supposed to mean something.

"Yeah…so?"

"That doesn't ring a bell?"

"Look, lady—" A pair of lanky kids ran up for autographs, stopping him from telling her to get to the point or get lost. He smiled, scrawled his name, jokingly asked them if they were bull riders. The question tickled them, like he knew it would, but mostly he wanted to drag out the conversation and annoy the proper and impatient Ms. Worthington.

"Is there someplace private we can talk?" she asked the second the kids ran off.

He spread his arms. "What's wrong with my office?"

"Funny." She didn't even crack a smile, only glanced around the parking lot. "I have a rental car. We can sit in there and not be interrupted."

"You still haven't told me what this is about. Hey, wait a minute— I know who you are. You guys make that crunchy green alien cereal, right?"

"Not exactly our claim to fame, but yes, one of our divisions is responsible for the Out of This World brand." She wrinkled her nose, and he hated to admit it, but she was kind of cute. "You'll recognize the name of a former subsidiary. Sundowner Leather Accessories."

"Oh, yeah, sure…they used to be one of my sponsors."

"Technically, they still are."

"I thought they went belly up."

"No. We chose to discontinue the line."

"Same thing." He shrugged. "Just a more polite way of saying someone screwed up."

She blinked, then continued to stare at him. "Where did you get your business degree, the local drugstore?"

"No kidding…you can get 'em there?" He grinned at her exasperated sigh.

Then he noticed two sweet young things standing off to the side, waiting, the taller one wearing a come-hither smile that eliminated the guesswork. Oh, yeah, maybe the night wouldn't end up a loss. But only if he could get rid of Mary Poppins here.

"Tell you what…" He brought his attention back to the Worthington woman, again caught off guard by the color of her eyes. "Is it Alex?"

"Alexis or Lexy. Either is fine."

"Okay, Lexy, how about I call you in a couple hours and we'll set something up?"

"Right," she drawled, glancing at the women. "Yeah, I'm not buying it."

"I'm offended." Rearing back, he gave her his best wounded expression. "You have my word."

She let out a surprisingly unladylike snort. "Still not buying it."

"Ma'am, a cowboy gives you his word, you can take it to the bank."

She laughed. "You're funny," she said, sizing him up again, then gesturing toward the women. "Go ahead. I'd like to see you in action."

Tanner stared at her. "You wanna what?"

"Come on, turn on the charm, give me a *ten* in the sex-appeal department." She slipped her sunglasses back on and shooed him with her other hand.

"Are you nuts?" He shook his head, not sure what he'd do if she didn't leave on her own. "That's rhetorical, by the way, because, lady, you are certifiable."

She smiled, her eyes now hidden behind the dark lenses. "Your fan club is starting to look bored. Better hurry."

The rodeo had ended and people were pouring out of the arena and into the parking lot. His window of opportunity was shrinking. Though in truth, he'd lost heart for chatting up the two young ladies.

It finally dawned on him. Lexy Worthington wasn't crazy, just manipulative. Determined. A potential pain in his ass. Better to get rid of her and be done with it. "All right, you win. What do you want?"

Her smile widened. "My rental is right over here."

"Can't you just spit it out?"

"I'd rather not," she said, her gaze sweeping the swelling crowd. "This is business, and discussing it out here would be inappropriate."

Unease itched the back of Tanner's neck. Maybe he was in trouble. If Sundowner really wasn't kaput he should still be wearing their logo on his shirt. He had on a belt they made and wondered if that counted.

Hell, his brother had brought the deal to him. Right after Doug had passed the bar exam, he'd negotiated the contract with a Sundowner bigwig. It hadn't amounted to much. But Doug had been eager to show his appreciation for Tanner's financial help so Tanner had rolled with it.

"All right," he said. "Lead the way."

She nodded, shifted the gigantic purse to her other hand and turned. "It's the white sedan right over—" She made a full circle, her gaze bouncing from one white car to the next. "This is absurd."

"Take it easy. It's a rental. Could happen to anybody."

"What could?"

"I'm assuming you don't know which sedan is yours."

She whipped off her sunglasses. "I'm wondering why so many people would buy bland white cars."

Tanner chuckled. "You remember the make?"

"It's domestic. I think." She looked at the plastic encased tag attached to the key. "Here's the plate number. Right?"

He took her wrist and turned her hand so he could see better. Her skin was really soft and she smelled awfully good. "Tell you what…let's go to my trailer, talk, have a beer. By then the lot will have thinned out and you can take whatever car's left."

Narrowing her gaze, she yanked back her hand. "I'm glad you find this so amusing."

He grinned. "No sense getting worked up over it. I have a fifth wheel sitting across the street. It's got plenty of room."

"First, what's a fifth wheel? And plenty of room for what?"

"Not what that warped mind of yours seems to have conjured." It tickled him the way her cute little nose went up in the air. "But I'm sure we can come to an agreement."

"Oh, we already have, Mr. Tanner," she said, suddenly all sweetness. "For the next ten days, I own your ass."

3

SURPRISE WASHED OVER Tanner's face, and Lexy tried not to react. She needed to take control of the situation and not waste the lifeline Norma had thrown her. Time was important. She was operating on a tight schedule and an even tighter budget. The longer it took her to drag his butt down to Houston for the photo shoot, the more money it would cost her. Money she didn't have. She didn't even have a credit card with wiggle room as backup. All because of her idiotic pride.

"Well, that explains it," he said, rubbing his shadowed jaw, his hazel eyes lit with amusement. "I saw you checking out my ass earlier. Seeing as how you think you own it, I understand why you felt the need to inspect it so closely."

She allowed for a small smile. If he thought he could ruffle her, he was in for another surprise. She slowly circled him, making a show of ogling his broad chest and muscled forearms. For good measure, she tilted her head to the side while she studied the seat of his worn jeans. "Yes, you'll do."

Watching her from over his shoulder, he lifted a dark brow. "You having fun?"

"Oh, I wouldn't call it that." She continued all the way

around while he tracked her with his interesting gold-and-green-flecked eyes.

He had a strong chiseled jaw the camera would love, with or without the few days' stubble. His brown hair was a bit long, touching the collar of his blue Western-style shirt. But it was a decent haircut and he had a great smile. It was possible she'd have to take him shopping before they showed up at the photo shoot, but by then her corporate credit card would have been issued. If not, she'd have to swallow her pride and hit up Norma for some cash. Something Lexy should've done in the first place.

She heard someone wolf whistle and looked up to see Tanner's mouth tighten. A pair of cowboys were walking by and laughing, the taller of the two giving Tanner a thumbs-up.

"Okay, that's enough," he muttered, tugging his hat lower. "We either finish this conversation in my trailer, or we can part company right now. The latter being my preference."

"Your trailer it is, then." She briefly reconsidered. A crowded parking lot might be the better option. Tanner was bound to give her a hard time. Probably flat out refuse to have anything to do with the calendar or the fragrance line. Just like most of the other rodeo cowboys. But unlike them, Tanner would be in breach of his contract if he refused to play nice. Unfortunately, she had the feeling a guy like him wouldn't care.

He started walking and she fell into step beside him. "Tell me straight up," he said, giving her a sidelong look. "Am I in hot water with you people?"

"Not that I'm aware. Why? Did you violate the indecency clause?" Dammit, she was warm.

"No. Maybe." He didn't look too happy, perhaps even a bit guilty. "Explain what that means and I'll let you know."

Lexy hid a smile. "How about you tell me what questionable behavior is bothering you and I'll let *you* know."

He snorted. "I might be a simple cowboy but I'm not stupid."

"I was teasing." Good to know he was concerned about violating his agreement. She had no idea if there was a decency clause, but she saw no reason to share that with him. No sense handing him ammunition to wiggle out of his contract.

"Oh…so that's you joking?" He mocked her with a pitying look. "You don't cut loose much, do you?"

Ha, she could shock him in that department. Playing loose was partly why she was here, overheated and wearing a suit she hated, worried about her maxed-out credit cards and holding her breath every time the warm breeze carried a whiff of horse dung. And now she was being punished instead of sitting in a cushy corner office on the top floor.

They stopped twice for Tanner to sign autographs for kids who bombarded him with questions. The women seemed to like him, too, flashing him smiles and giving him suggestive looks that he fielded like a man accustomed to feminine attention. That was good, excellent. Lexy had seen several headshots of the men already lined up for the calendar. Tanner would have some stiff competition.

While he signed, she thought about taking a couple pictures of him against the stunning background of the Rockies. The hills leading up to the snow-capped peaks were as green as emeralds and would really show off his eyes.

Before she could get out her phone, he finished with the boys and was promptly intercepted by a cowboy trying to get Tanner to join a late-night poker game. He shook his head and kept walking until they reached a trailer parked behind a late-model motor coach. In fact, all the other RVs in the park were much nicer than Tanner's. He opened the trailer door and didn't even flinch at the annoying creak.

"I can't recall how I left things. So enter at your own risk," he said, yanking off his Stetson with a sweeping gesture for her to go first.

If he was trying to scare her off he'd be disappointed. She'd spent time in too many frat houses to worry about when she'd gotten her last tetanus shot. The first step was a tad wobbly, but she ignored the hand he offered and made it inside.

The place was roomier and neater than she'd expected. Though the kitchen and living areas were small, they were well laid out with appliances, cabinets and built-in furniture. At the far back she could see part of a bed.

"Home sweet home," Tanner said, crowding in behind her, near enough for her to feel the heat from his body. "Ever been in one of these?"

"No," she murmured, unsure which direction to go to give him room.

"I didn't think so."

"What does that mean?" She turned around to look at him, finding out too late he was even closer than she'd imagined. She bumped his chest with her right breast, then made everything worse by clutching his muscled arm for support.

He took it as a cue to put a hand on her waist. "You okay?"

"Fine." She looked into his hazel eyes, the oddest thought niggling at her. He smelled good. Even though he shouldn't, not after having ridden a bronc. The scent was vaguely familiar, an unexpectedly wonderful combination of leather and something spicy.

She leaned closer, her eyes drifting closed on a deep inhale. When she opened them, she found him staring at her.

"It's kind of stuffy in here," he said, his voice lower and rougher. "Why don't you take off your jacket while I open windows?"

Her fingers were still wrapped around his arm, the tips digging into the hard, muscled flesh. She jerked back her hand. He seemed reluctant to remove his from her waist, letting his palm slide to her hip before he withdrew altogether.

"What is that cologne you're wearing?" she asked, retreating into business mode and breaking eye contact. Feeling like an idiot, she moved to the small brown couch. "I can't quite make out the scent."

"Cologne?" He said it as if it were a cussword, prompting her to look at him again. He was fiddling with a window, and her gaze went straight to his butt. The man filled out a pair of jeans quite well…both front and back. "I wouldn't wear that crap if you paid me."

That snapped her out of her preoccupation. "Well, that's a problem." She really did need to lose her jacket before she passed out from heatstroke.

"How so?" After forcing the window open, he turned to her, his gaze lingering on her breasts as she struggled out of the blazer.

She could hardly object after staring at his ass. Which she unabashedly did again when he bent to bring two beers out of the fridge. He twisted off the cap and held one out to her.

"No, thanks. Water or iced tea would be great, though." She glanced around for a place to hang the jacket, then just draped it over the arm of the couch.

He'd exchanged the unopened beer for a bottle of water that he passed to her. While she took a sip, he tipped the beer to his lips.

"Take the couch," he said, straddling a chair at the table. "Stick to the right side. There's a lump on the left."

She twisted around to check it out before she sat.

"It's clean."

"That's not what I was—" She sighed and sank into the cushion. This was the good side?

"You wanted to talk. I'm listening."

Lexy met his watchful eyes. They seemed darker now, more green than gold, and for all his easygoing manner, she had the impression that he missed very little of what went on around him.

"I have something I need you to do. *We*," she quickly amended. "The Worthington Group."

"My contract was with Sundowner."

"Your contract is actually with the holding company, and we have you for ten more days."

"Ah, you own my ass I believe is how you referred to my indenture."

Lexy smiled at the term he'd chosen. He possessed his own brand of charm and she could see why women found him attractive. Perhaps this silly errand wouldn't be as big a pain as she'd expected. "Yes, that might have been an overly ambitious statement. However, it seemed appropriate at the moment."

His slow grin made her heart speed up. He took another pull of beer, his eyes staying on her face even as his head went back. He lowered the bottle, then used the back of his wrist to wipe his damp mouth. "Where are you from?"

"Oklahoma."

His brows went up. "Born and raised?"

She nodded. "Outside of Oklahoma City. Why do you seem surprised?"

Tanner's broad shoulders moved in a slight shrug. "Your family ever been ranchers?"

"Quite a few generations back. Then they struck oil and eventually branched out into several different businesses." Hard as it was to believe, he honestly didn't seem familiar with the far-reaching Worthington Group. Most people would recognize the name. "I'll get to the point. We'll be introducing a men's fragrance line next year and we're looking for a spokesperson."

She paused to take a sip of water. A second later, her stomach rumbled loudly, but she willed herself not to react. When she looked at Tanner again, it was as if another man had taken his place.

His mouth had pulled into a tight, thin line. Wariness and scorn darkened his eyes. "So…what's it to me?"

"I'm not saying we're asking you to be that person but—"

"Good." He stood and started unbuttoning his shirt.

"What are you doing?"

"I'm gonna take a shower. Wanna join me?"

"Oh, so we're back to you trying to scare me off." So interested in his smooth, muscled chest, she almost missed his cocky smile.

"Definitely not what I had in mind." He deliberately ran a gaze down her front. "Why not have a little fun before you go?"

"I'm not going anywhere without you."

"Wanna bet?"

Lexy thought for a moment. Of course he was only taunting her but it could work in her favor. "Sure. Five hundred bucks. Unless that's too rich for you."

He got to the last button and yanked the shirt from his jeans. "I'd feel real bad taking advantage of you."

"Oh, don't worry about that." She sounded too confident, she realized. The goal was to win that five hundred off him. Later she'd give it back, tell him she'd been joking, but she could use the cash now. Dear God…what had become of her? Her father would just— "Do we have a bet?"

He shrugged out of his shirt and she had to watch. He had a fine chest. Great shoulders, too, well-defined muscles bunching and releasing with the movement of his arms. When her gaze finally made it back to his face, he looked a little suspicious.

"You know I didn't mean an actual bet," he said, walking

past her to drop his shirt into a basket near the bed. "But you seem all fired-up sure you can take five large off me. That's got me curious."

"And worried."

He let out a short laugh. "Nothing you can say or do will make me pimp your perfume."

"Men's cologne."

"Hell, call it whatever you want."

"You haven't even heard the details." She'd noticed the three-inch surgical scar on the back of his shoulder. The other one below his ribs was jagged and definitely not left by a surgeon's knife.

"Don't need to." Tanner unbuckled his belt.

"Really?" She leaned back, got comfortable and stared at his fly. Oh, he did not want to play chicken with her.

His only answer was to unsnap his jeans and pull the zipper down halfway.

"Let's see what you got. I should know what I'm peddling."

He narrowed his eyes, then laughed. "I knew you were a whack job from the get-go. I should've ditched you in the parking lot."

"Yet here we are."

Tanner studied her face, the amusement gone, replaced by annoyance. As though he couldn't figure her out. "Last chance."

She smiled and kicked off her shoes.

He unzipped the rest of the way, and receiving no re-action, pulled off his jeans. She hoped he couldn't see her holding her breath and didn't notice her relief when she saw the brown boxer-briefs. If he'd gone commando, she wasn't sure what she would've done. No, not true. She would've stayed where she was, cool as could be. That's what she chose to think, anyway. Because staring at him in the body-molding underwear wasn't easy, either.

Will Tanner was really…something. No spare flesh, just muscle. His thighs, butt, calves, his…Lexy silently cleared her throat. The man was quite well-endowed.

"Very good," she said, grateful her voice didn't crack or climb several octaves. But damn, she had to stop looking. She pulled out her phone and concentrated on the screen, flipping from one picture to the next. "You should have no trouble getting a month on the calendar."

He flung his jeans at the bed, then faced her full on. "The what?"

"The promotional calendar that will debut the fragrance and decide the spokesperson. Didn't I mention it?" She looked up, undaunted by his dark, menacing expression. "We want you to be Mr. October."

HE STARED IN stunned silence, and then laughed. "Who put you up to this? Charlie?"

"Um, no one. I'm really here on behalf of The Worthington Group."

"I should've known right off." Tanner shook his head, taking in her shapely calves and slim ankles. "You have too nice a body to wear that frumpy outfit."

Her eyebrows arched with just the right amount of indignation. She was good. "This is an Armani suit."

His birthday was in four weeks. Charlie always got the day right but not the month. Usually they just had a drink, but Charlie was probably trying to make a point that it was time for Tanner to follow him into retirement. He folded his arms across his chest and leaned against the bathroom doorjamb. "Go ahead. Skip to the part where you pull your hair loose and take off your clothes."

She blinked, glanced at his chest, then let her head fall back, her lips slowly forming a smile as she stared at the ceiling. "This is just perfect," she murmured to herself, then brought her head up. "I don't know anyone named Charlie and I'm not a stripper."

He kind of hoped that wasn't true. It wasn't only her pretty blue eyes that had stirred his interest. She had nice legs and breasts. He hadn't seen her backside without the jacket yet, but he doubted he'd be disappointed.

"I won't tell Charlie I guessed early. You go on and do your little act, darlin'. I promise I'll enjoy it just as much as if it had been a surprise," he said, extending a hand to help her off the couch.

She swatted him away. "You jackass. I am not a stripper."

"I never said you were. I forget what they call people like you."

"Pissed off." She reached into that gigantic purse of hers and he expected music to start playing. Instead, she yanked out her wallet, then leaned back and studied him. "Are you putting me on? You can't really think—" She sighed and flipped open the brown leather billfold. "Here."

He took it, saw she had an Oklahoma driver's license and hadn't lied about her name. Before handing it back to her, he noticed that she was twenty-eight. "Well, damn, I was real fond of the stripper idea."

"Now, will you put some clothes on so we can finish our conversation?"

He could feel the dust in his hair and the grit clinging to the back of his neck. "After I take my shower."

She glanced at her watch, something she did a lot. Obviously she had somewhere else to be, which suited him fine if she was gonna keep harping on that men's fragrance bullshit. "All right," she said, "but you'll need to hurry."

"Yeah, I'll do that." He grabbed a towel off the shelf, then paused at the bathroom door. "You're still welcome to join me."

She rolled her eyes then started messing with her phone.

Grinning, Tanner ducked his head and entered the tiny bathroom. He'd had the trailer for going on ten years now, and sure, he would've preferred a bigger shower. And the bed was barely long enough. Some of the guys had teased him about holding on to the fifth wheel instead of getting something bigger and newer, especially after his two-year winning streak. Nah, he and Betsy had done just fine. She'd never given him a lick of trouble and she'd already outlasted two trucks. But then he'd never been the type who had to have the newest and brightest toy. New gadgets just made his head hurt.

Waiting for the water to warm up, he hung his towel, made sure he had enough shampoo and peeled off his underwear. He stuck his head out. She was still busy with her phone, texting, by the looks of it. Her hair wasn't as tidy as before. Long loose curls fell around her face. The late sun came through the open window and picked up the shiny gold highlights.

She moved and the sunlight hit her face, glistening off her pale peach lips. His body's reaction shouldn't have surprised him. She was much prettier than he'd first thought. And his cock was definitely interested.

"Hey, Lexy." He waited until she looked up. "I'll leave the door open in case you change your mind."

She ran a quick gaze over what she could see of his chest. "Yeah…thanks." She smiled. "Not going to happen."

Chuckling, he left the door partially open just to be ornery, then slipped under the spray. The warm water felt good on his tired muscles. He'd ridden in this annual rodeo every June for five years now and liked this particular trailer park. Not just for the convenient location but because of the water pressure. Pretty sad when he stopped to think about it. At the end of the day, a man ought to have more than a great shower to look forward to.

Man, he could probably write a travel guide to the best

and worst parks from Montana down to the Tex/Mex border. Although except for a handful, they blurred together. It sure was gonna be weird when he finally quit and put down roots. Wherever that ended up being. At least he'd finally narrowed it down to a choice between two places.

Quickly he shampooed his hair, soaped up, then rinsed off. Ordinarily, he liked to spend a good fifteen minutes under the warm spray, but his thoughts had strayed back to Lexy. If she wasn't here for some birthday bump and grind, he had to believe she was here on Worthington business just like she claimed. Which meant she probably wasn't fooling about the calendar.

Shit.

That would be the damn day he'd stoop so low.

Kind of a shame that he had to get rid of her, but so be it. He reached for the faucet, twisted wrong and aggravated his strained shoulder muscle. He let out a loud groan before he could stop himself.

"Are you all right?"

Ignoring her, Tanner gingerly grabbed the towel from the hook and stepped out of the stall. He dried his face first. Then lowered the towel and saw her standing in the doorway, staring.

4

"OH." LEXY DID an abrupt about-face. Lightheaded from lack of food, she flattened her hand against the wall. What on earth had she been thinking? People tended not to shower with their clothes on. Of course he was naked.

"You're not gonna faint, are you?"

She heard the laugh in his voice. It didn't help alleviate her embarrassment. "I'm sorry. I heard you groan and I thought maybe you were—" Oh, God, what if he hadn't groaned. What if he'd been…moaning? "I don't know what I thought," she murmured, wishing she could disappear.

"It's okay. No harm done. You can turn around now."

"Are you dressed?"

"Sort of."

Her cheeks were burning. She still felt a little woozy. The last thing she'd eaten were the early-morning cheese crackers at the Will Rogers Airport.

"I'm assuming you've seen a naked man before."

"No. Never." She pushed away from the wall and turned around. "I'm single."

Tanner wore a grin on his face and a towel wrapped around his hips. That was it. "You're pretty good," he said. "Remind me not to invite you to a poker game."

"I'm not lying. Where I come from lots of women and

men take purity pledges. We're saving ourselves for marriage." She kept her eyes level with his, as if she couldn't bear to look down at all his nakedness. She threw in a bit of lower-lip nibbling. The drama classes she'd taken to spite her father seemed to have paid off.

Tanner's wavering smile and uncertain frown gave her some satisfaction. "I've got to get to my clothes," he said, motioning that she needed to move.

"Yes, of course." She averted her gaze, mostly to keep from bursting into laughter, then kept her head down all the way back to the couch. The trouble was, she wanted another peek before he got dressed. "We don't have a lot of time," she said and glanced toward the bed. But he'd already put the dividing wall between them. "Our flight is in three hours. I'm assuming you can leave your trailer here?"

Several long seconds later she understood the term "deafening silence" on a whole new level.

"Our flight?" He emerged from behind the wall, zipping up a fresh pair of jeans. No shirt. No boots. His hair damp and messy. "First of all, I'm not going anywhere with you. More to the point, I don't fly."

"It's a commercial plane. It's not as if I'm asking you to take a puddle-jumper."

"I don't care what you call it. If it's got wings and leaves the ground, I don't set foot on it."

"Oh, please. Now I know you're baiting me. Who doesn't fly in this day and age?"

He jerked a thumb at his very nice chest. "Me." She watched wistfully as he grabbed a black T-shirt. "I'm not alone. A lot of people don't fly. You and your little purity circle probably have your own set of back-up wings, so no problem for you all."

That almost made her laugh so she was glad he pulled the shirt over his head. Though she'd miss the view. The man took care of himself, the ridges of muscle across his belly and shoulders nicely defined but not bulky.

"Have you tried a mild tranquilizer?" she asked. "You know, say, an hour before a flight."

Walking past her, he grabbed his beer. "I'll save both of us a whole lot of time. No. That's your blanket answer for the next two minutes, or however long it takes for you to get your cute little backside out of my trailer."

"You don't know what I'm going to ask."

"Don't care. It'll all come down to *no* in the end."

"Sorry, but you don't have that option."

He rinsed the bottle, dropped it in a receptacle and glanced out the window. "The parking lot is almost empty. Your rental should be easy to find."

Her patience slipped. She didn't have time to baby him. "Did you ever read your contract with Sundowner?"

"Course I read it," he muttered, turning to frown at her. "At least my attorney did."

"As an aside, you might think about hiring a new one. Because he left you wide open."

"What do you mean?"

"The minute you signed, you didn't only climb into bed with Sundowner but with every arm of The Worthington Group. Which meant you agreed not to accept sponsorship from any company considered a competitor. That list is quite long."

Animosity darkened his face. "Nice business you work for. Or own."

"I don't own any of it." She had to look away. The contract had been horribly one-sided, nothing she would've participated in, but that wasn't stopping her from using it to her advantage. "Perhaps your anger would be better directed at your attorney. The agreement also means you can't turn down the photo shoot."

"You let me worry about my attorney," he said, the curtness in his tone luring her gaze back to him. He stared out the window, the tic at his jaw working frantically. "You'd mentioned the contract expires in ten days."

"Yes, that's true."

"This promotion thing you're doing can't possibly be wrapped up that soon."

"No, but if you're selected as the spokesperson, the offer will be quite lucrative and—"

"I don't give a shit about the money." He turned a glare on her. "I'm not the guy for this fragrance crap. You have to know that," he said, his expression easing as he spread his hands. "There's a new crop of ambitious, young cowboys out there making names for themselves. Go talk to them. I guarantee you'll find at least one who'll be willing to hawk your cologne."

Dammit, she was feeling guiltier by the minute. She couldn't tell him he was a last resort. "I'm afraid they— *we* want someone with a couple championships under his belt. A man who, like yourself, has been with professional rodeo awhile and has a name—"

He muttered a curse. "Even without a fancy business degree I know that any one of those young bucks with their Facebook and Twitter and whatever else they use would be a lot more marketable than a guy like me."

"Not necessarily."

"Come on. You're a smart woman. You've done your homework. Five years ago I was the winning ticket. Now?" He shrugged a shoulder. But his reaction was in no way nonchalant. His jaw had tightened and he wouldn't look at her. "I'm months, maybe weeks away from calling it quits. Saying adios to rodeo."

"Seriously?"

He swung a puzzled frown at her. "I'm scoring low, spending more money than I'm winning, had two surgeries already and I'm thirty-three. Getting too old for this game."

"Lots of guys older than you are still riding," she said, hating the trace of defeat in his voice.

Tanner reacted as if she'd slapped him. Plowing a hand through his hair, he brushed past without looking at her. "It happens to everyone sooner or later so do me the courtesy of dropping the pity."

"I wasn't…" Lexy closed her mouth, aware she couldn't trust herself not to confess it was guilt, not pity that she felt.

She breathed in deeply, really despising what this trip had come to. Why she'd imagined getting Tanner to Houston would be easy, she had no idea. Part of the problem was that she hadn't expected to like him. She'd left Oklahoma City assuming he'd be just another cowboy like the ones who'd already turned down the proposition, except Tanner had no choice. He'd honor his contract by doing what she told him, then they'd part ways, and that would be that.

But she did like him, and yes, there was a little bit of pity roiling inside her, yet she was forcing him to do something he strongly objected to only so she could prove herself. Actually, this foolishness proved nothing. It was her father's petty way of humbling her. So they were both using Tanner.

No, this was on her. She could stop this charade right now. Refuse to exploit the lousy contract his attorney had been too stupid or lazy to negotiate.

She watched a very grim Tanner sit on the edge of his bed and pull on his boots. If only she could explain to him that all he had to do was show for the photo shoot. She'd be forever grateful and he could walk away free and clear. After she got paid, perhaps she could even give him some money for his trouble. The thought made her uneasy. He wouldn't appreciate the offer. He'd said he didn't care about money, and she believed him.

Her maxed-out credit cards and unpaid student-loan notices flashed before her eyes. Unfortunately, right now, money was her key motivation. "Whether you have any interest in the calendar or not, you understand that you must show up for the photo shoot. If nothing else, it's a good-faith effort on your part."

"See, I don't get that. I'm telling you I want nothing to do with your new cologne, and the second my contract expires I'm done. So why waste everyone's time?"

She shrugged. "Don't shoot the messenger."

His lips moved, and though she couldn't hear him, she could well imagine what he was muttering to himself. He tugged the hem of his jeans over his boots and stood.

A glance at her watch made her breath catch. "I brought a copy of your contract in case you had questions." They couldn't afford to miss their flight. Staying over a night translated to expenses her credit card couldn't cover. "If you have trouble with the legalese, your attorney will verify what I'm saying."

Every time she mentioned his attorney Tanner looked as if he wanted to strangle her. She didn't understand what that was about but she kept quiet, pulled the folder out of her purse and passed it to him.

He stared at it. "I remember one thing. You people agreed not to interfere with my riding schedule. I have two events coming up. No way I can make it to Houston and back in time."

"Where are you scheduled to ride?"

"Iowa."

Tempted as she was to ask him the date, she already knew he was playing loose with the truth and making him more defensive wouldn't help her cause. "That's a month from now."

"Yeah, but there's Wyoming before that."

"No." She shook her head. "I already checked."

"How?"

She held up her phone. "Online."

"But…" He looked confused, angry and maybe even embarrassed because she'd caught him lying. "You couldn't have checked every rodeo lineup."

"I didn't. I looked up your name on Google. If you'd like, I'll show you what comes up."

"Jesus." He glared at her phone as if it were the enemy. And then looked at her the same way. "A man can't have privacy anymore." He tossed the folder on the couch and then picked up a magazine off the side table and looked underneath. Next he dug into a plastic bin filled with packaged cookies and crackers.

He found his phone, an older model that she doubted had internet capability. She watched him hit speed dial and hoped he was calling his attorney. Maybe then Tanner would understand that he had no choice, and they could still make the flight paid for out of the corporate account. Same thing for the car. Anything that deviated from the plan would cost her money she didn't have.

She went to the window and glanced at the parking lot across the street. Finding the rental wouldn't be a problem, but she wanted to give him some privacy. Or at least the illusion of privacy. "Doug, call me as soon as you get this," Tanner said. "It's important."

Dammit. He'd obviously had to leave a message. If he stubbornly waited to talk to the attorney, she'd be screwed. "I'm assuming that's your lawyer. Does he return calls promptly?"

Ignoring her, Tanner hit another number. He drummed his long, tanned fingers on the counter while he waited, not once sparing her a glance. "Helen," he said, his tone more pleasant. "You're right, darlin'. I can smell that cherry pie clear up to Montana." He paused. "You know where Doug is?" Squeezing his eyes shut, he pinched the bridge of his nose. "How long?" Tanner sighed and stared past her toward the window. "I already left one, but if you hear from him, tell him he's gotta call me ASAP."

By the way he fidgeted, it was obvious he was impatient to get off the phone, but his voice never gave him away. Lexy assumed Helen was the attorney's assistant, and Tanner exchanged several more pleasantries with her before he disconnected the call and flung the phone on the couch.

While Lexy waited for the temper in his eyes to settle, she moved to look at the pictures he had taped to his fridge. She suspected it might take a while. He kept rubbing the back of his neck and for a second glanced at the contract copy she'd brought but he made no move to pick it up.

Reminding herself patience was her only ally at the moment, she leaned in for a closer look at the pictures. The more faded photo was of a mountain lake, the other was taken on a beach with a fishing pole stuck in the white sand. That was it. No people were in either photo.

"Give me your number," he said finally. "I'll call you as soon as I hear from Doug."

"When do you expect that to be?"

"No idea. He's on vacation in the Bahamas."

She nearly choked. "Oh, no. No. Uh-uh." She shook her head, paused, told herself to breathe. "No. We can't wait around."

"Take it easy." Curiosity flickered in his eyes. "He'll call me back."

"But we have a flight to catch."

"Look, no matter what happens, I'm not getting on a plane. So get that out of your head."

She took another deep breath to counter the panic tightening her chest. "You really can't fly? It's not just a ploy?"

"Nope."

God help her, he was telling the truth. Her brain's mad scramble in search of a solution made her dizzy again. More likely it was her empty stomach. She hurried to the couch and fished in her purse for a mint or hard candy.

"You okay?"

"I will be."

"You look kinda pale."

"I haven't eaten since early this morning. I need a sugar boost." She found a peppermint disc that she tried to unwrap but her hands shook.

"How about orange juice?" He didn't wait for an answer but brought a jug out of the fridge.

"This is so stupid. Dammit." Why couldn't she get the dumb wrapper off?

"Here." He swapped the candy for a glass of juice.

She accepted it with both hands, afraid the tumbler might slip. If the tremor wasn't bad enough, now her palms were clammy.

Tanner sat next to her on the couch. He wrapped a hand around hers and helped guide the juice to her mouth.

Embarrassed, she took a tiny sip, then tried to break away from him. "I'm okay. Thanks."

"Can you take a bigger one?" he asked, his roughened fingertips gentle on her skin as he urged the glass back to her lips.

She could smell him again, the same mysterious mix of leather and spice with the added hint of soap. It must be his shampoo that smelled so good. The heat from his body warmed her, making her drowsy and stirring the impulse to lay her head on his shoulder. It seemed like a lifetime ago since she'd had a decent night's sleep. Always worrying about money and bills. He waited patiently for her to drink more of the juice before he slackened his hand and let her lower the glass.

"You could be coming down with something." He pressed the back of his fingers to her cheek much like a mother would do to her feverish child.

"I'm not." Lexy laughed, leaning away from him. "I'm really not."

He lowered his hand and stood. "I didn't mean to get in your face. Old habit. Sorry."

"Do you have kids?" she asked, the sudden thought oddly disturbing.

"Nah, a younger brother. He kept me up more than a few nights. You feeling better yet?"

She nodded, then chugged down more of the juice . "No flying, huh?"

Tanner folded his arms across his chest. "You can ask me a hundred times but it won't change my answer."

Lexy swept a gaze toward the back. Only one bed and the couch was lumpy. But what choice did she have? "Then I guess we drive."

WHILE HE WAITED for her to turn in the rental car, Tanner tried his brother again. And again, no answer. But at least he got to leave a more satisfying message. Much as he still wanted to strangle Lexy, he hadn't been willing to use certain cusswords in front of her.

He watched her leave the rental office carrying a bag she'd taken from the trunk. Years of conditioning made him want to jump out and help her with it, but he forced himself to stay behind the wheel of his truck. No sense making things easier for her. What he needed was for her to recognize this standoff between them for what it was, cut her losses and let him be.

The crazy thing was she had to know he'd try to run the clock on his contract. So much could happen on a road trip, even if he didn't stoop to sabotage. Which he wasn't above doing if it came down to the wire. And he'd wager she knew that, too. So why the dogged determination?

He tensed when he saw her stop and use the back of her wrist to blot her forehead. Two hours until sunset but it was still warm, and she'd had nothing but the orange juice. She shifted the bag to her other hand.

"Shit." Tanner opened his door and got out. His longer strides closed the distance between them before she made it two steps.

"What are you doing?"

Without a word, he took the bag from her. It wasn't heavy but he felt better giving in. No, he wasn't happy with this new thorn in his backside but he didn't have to be a bastard. Rather than opening the trailer, he stowed the bag on the truck's backseat. Lexy watched for a moment, probably making sure he hadn't tossed her things in the bushes. Then she went around to the passenger side.

He followed her in case she needed help getting into the cab. The step-up wasn't easy for someone short. She just stood there as if making the climb was too much for her, and he revisited the notion that she might be playing him. Trying to gain his sympathy while she dug in her claws. But then he saw that she'd only stopped to take off her blazer.

She turned her head and caught him eyeing her flat belly and jutting breasts. "Did you need something?"

"You want help getting up there?" he asked, motioning with his chin.

Draping the jacket over her arm, she inspected the step-up. "I think I'll be fine." She flashed him a smile. "But thank you."

He managed to get behind the wheel before she settled into her seat, and tried not to notice the lacy pink bra exposed by the gap in her blouse. "It's not too late," he said, looking straight ahead and turning the key. "You can still fly to Houston and I'll meet you there."

"No, I think we should stick to our plan."

Our plan, his ass. His first choice had been to drop her off at the airport. Second, he'd suggested she keep the rental and follow him. But no, she'd insisted on sticking as close as possible. And when he'd told her he wouldn't negotiate, she'd threatened him. Asked him if he could afford being hit with a lawsuit for breach of contract.

Oh, she'd looked contrite as all get-out, explained it wasn't her decision. Personally, she would never take legal action against him. He still wasn't sure he believed her. His brother would be able to advise him. Though Doug hadn't done such a bang-up job on the contract terms. And with all the money Tanner had doled out for law school. Yeah, that pissed him off.

As soon as he'd gotten them on the highway, he glanced over at her. "You really think your company would sue me?"

"I don't know. Probably." She turned to look out her window. "They have quite an impressive legal department."

"You always say *they*. You're a Worthington. Isn't it your company, too?"

Her smile seemed forced. "My father runs The Worthington Group."

"Not fond of the old man, huh?"

"That's not true." She shot him a withering look. "Why would you say such a thing?"

Tanner set cruise control and leaned back. "Your body language."

"Pay attention to the road and not me."

He laughed when she flapped a hand, motioning for him to move the arm he'd stretched out behind her head, even though he wasn't touching her. "Okay, sore subject. I get it. I'm not fond of my old man, either."

"I didn't say— I'm not engaging in this conversation with you." She folded her arms across her chest, hiding the gap…and pink bra. "Oh, wait, I don't have to explain. You being such an ace at body language."

"You need something in that belly of yours. Maybe some food will give you a more pleasing disposition."

Lexy slid him a long look. "I'm fine. We need to make

use of the daylight." She took out her phone and started working away. "I assume I won't have internet the whole time we're on the road. Do you have a map?"

"What for?"

"Um, the usual purpose. Figure out where we're going."

Tanner smiled. "Don't you worry. I know exactly where we're headed."

And she damn sure wasn't gonna like it.

5

A BUMP WOKE LEXY. She opened her eyes but it was already dark, not even a hint of moonlight to help her get her bearings. The truck had been a surprisingly smooth ride but she felt the uneven change in the road and guessed they'd left the highway.

"Where are we?" She saw a blurry glow up ahead. "Is that the trailer park?" She picked up her phone from where she'd dropped it on her lap, held it up and flipped on her Bic app.

Tanner swung a sharp look at the flickering light. "Is that—you've got to be kidding."

"What?" The truck's headlights bounced off trees and shrubs flanking the narrow stretch of road. Gasping, she clutched her armrest when a reflective pair of eyes appeared directly in front of them.

Tanner protectively flung his arm out as he slammed the brakes. Her upper body lurched forward in spite of her fastened seat belt. They stopped short of hitting the startled doe, but it took Lexy a few moments to calm down from the near miss. And the fact that her breasts were pressed against Tanner's muscled arm.

She touched his hand. "I'm all right. Thanks."

His alert gaze had remained on the deer, who still hadn't

moved. He slowly turned his head, saw the problem and lowered his arm. "She's got her baby with her," he said, returning his attention to the animal.

"Where?"

"Right there next to that juniper tree." He leaned close, using his chin to guide her. "That fawn isn't more than a few weeks old."

Seconds later her vision adjusted to the murky shadows that hid the little one. "Oh, she's adorable." A sick feeling threatened to ruin the moment. "We almost killed her mother."

"But we didn't." He looked at Lexy, his face unnervingly close. Gradually, he leaned back to his side. "I was going slow. This kind of thing isn't unusual out here. You just have to drive cautiously and keep your eyes peeled."

"Why do they do that? Of course I've heard the deer-caught-in-the-headlights saying, but I would think their basic instinct would be to run in another direction."

He shrugged. "It's also instinctual for animals to protect their young. For the four-legged variety, anyway," he said with a hint of cynicism, enough to draw her gaze back to him. Someone had disappointed Will Tanner. "Maybe she somehow knew they couldn't both make it across in time." The corners of his mouth lifted. "There they go."

Lexy thought of her own father. Why hadn't her return, hat in hand, been enough to allow him to play the magnanimous parent while he privately gloated? He'd sent her on this ridiculous errand to what end? If it hadn't been for Norma, Lexy doubted she could've found the right cowboy in such a short period of time.

And if she'd failed, would he have turned his back on her? None of it made sense. Her father did not stick his nose into anything so trivial. For that matter, the whole fragrance line seemed fishy. But it was Harrison's project and maybe dear old Dad wanted to make sure they could play nice together.

The doe waited for her fawn, much like a mom would show her child how to use a crosswalk. It was really sweet, watching the pair until they disappeared into the brush. Lexy couldn't recall the last time she'd felt a surge of gratitude for such a simple yet special moment. She leaned back against the headrest and closed her eyes as Tanner put the truck in gear and they slowly moved forward.

Lexy straightened with a jerk. "Oh, my God, I was asleep."

"Yes, you were," he agreed, the amusement in his voice clearly intended to tease her.

But she didn't care if she'd snored or even drooled. This was major. "For how long?"

"A couple of hours."

She stared at the dashboard clock, trying to remember when she'd last been aware of the time. "I don't usually nod off like that."

"I'm honored to have that effect on you."

"No, really, I have horrible insomnia. I can't sleep since I—" She bit down on her lip. What was wrong with her? She'd been about to confide in a virtual stranger. Her money problems were her own. "Has your attorney called?"

"No." His terse response brought them back to even ground.

She stared into the darkness. "When we stop, I'd be happy to go over the contract with you." A yawn snuck up on her, and she snuggled down in the seat again. Who knew a truck could be this comfortable? "Wait a minute." She brought her head up. "Where are we?"

"Minutes away from our destination."

"Which is?" She didn't like the cheery note in his voice or the ambiguous answer.

"The Lone Wolf."

Interesting name for a trailer park. It was also quite out of the way. She found the map on her phone. "What town are we in?"

"We drove through Blackfoot Falls fifteen minutes ago."

She covered another yawn, then blinked at the map. "No, can't be. That would mean we went west. We're headed south."

"Eventually, we'll do just that. Tonight we're staying with my friend Matt."

"No." She glared at Tanner. "No, you can't do this."

"Do what? Sleep? Matt's got a couple of guest rooms for us. I talked to him an hour ago."

"We had a plan. A schedule. You can't just—"

"No, *you* had a plan. Me, I have business with Matt."

"This isn't fair," she said, trying to hold on to her temper.

"Damn right, it isn't. You hijack a man and then expect him to drop everything and jump to it. This ain't your rodeo. You don't like it, I'll stop the truck and you can walk back to town. Say the word."

Lexy pressed her lips together. She believed him. Oh, she doubted he'd make her walk. But he'd love the excuse to drop her off in town and be rid of her. What she didn't doubt was that that would be the last she'd see of Will Tanner.

UNSURE HOW SHE should handle this new twist, Lexy hovered near the truck, parked several yards from a two-story house. It was a large, older, well-maintained home with lots of stone accents, shutters and beige trim around the windows. Behind her were stables, barns, corrals and other outbuildings. The Lone Wolf was quite a spread.

Seconds after Tanner had clapped the brass knocker, the red door opened and a couple close to her age greeted him. She knew their names and that was about it.

"Good to see you again, Rachel." He kissed the woman's cheek, then shook Matt's hand. "You two set a date yet?"

Rachel shook her head, and Matt nodded.

Tanner laughed. "That seems about right."

"He doesn't understand that planning a wedding isn't that simple." Rachel flipped her hair over her shoulder, the long auburn curls catching the porch light.

"You call the Justice of the Peace, show up when he tells you to and say I do." Matt spread his hands. "How is that hard?"

"I'm the only daughter. You know I can't do that to my mom." Rachel looked past Tanner and smiled at Lexy, who pretended to fish a pebble out of her shoe. "Come in, everyone. Tanner, introduce us to your friend."

He turned to her with a faint smile that she knew meant he was about to annoy her. "If she'll hurry and get her cute little behind over here, I will. Honey, what was your name again?" His grin broadened at her stony expression, then he turned back to Matt. "These buckle bunnies," he said, "hard to keep them straight."

Rachel's mouth opened but nothing came out. She apparently didn't know Tanner well enough to judge if he was joking or not.

"Oh, man, a bronc must've kicked you in the head today." Matt moved back into the foyer, smothering a laugh. "You're gonna get it from both of them for that."

"Jeez, Tanner." Rachel huffed. "Matt didn't tell me you were a jerk."

Lexy liked her immediately and decided she'd go inside after all. "I didn't mean to be rude..." she said, extending her hand to both of them and completely ignoring Tanner. "I'm Alexis."

"I'm Rachel McAllister. Come on in." She had a friendly smile and mischievous green eyes. "We'll go have something cold to drink while these two jokers take your bags upstairs."

"Oh, no." Lexy should've foreseen this would be awkward. "Not my bag, but thank you."

Rachel barely blinked. "All right, but you'll come inside?"

"Sure." Lexy slid Tanner a glance. His arms were folded, his hat pulled low and shadowing his face. She wished she could see his expression better. Okay, she didn't really think he'd take off without her, but… "Coming?"

"In a minute."

She hesitated, then Matt slipped past her to join Tanner. Knowing Matt would be out here with him put her at ease.

Rachel led her to the surprisingly modern kitchen with its blue-pearl granite countertops.

"Have a seat," Rachel said, gesturing to an older oak table with matching chairs that seemed out of place with the gleaming steel appliances. "We have iced tea, soda, beer, wine or I can make coffee."

Lexy was tempted by the wine but decided she'd better stick to something that would keep her alert. "Iced tea sounds wonderful."

"Sweet?"

"Please."

Rachel smiled. "I went to school in Dallas. Everyone seems to love sweet tea there."

"In Oklahoma, too. At least my family members are devotees. I attended college in California and a lot of people there thought I was nuts."

For the next ten minutes, they drank tea and made small talk, Lexy surprised to learn that the seemingly urbane Rachel had grown up on a spread not far from the Lone Wolf. Even more unexpected, she'd returned to Montana to marry Matt and help him run the family ranch.

When the two men joined them, Lexy noticed how Rachel's eyes lit up at the sight of Matt. He kissed the top of her head and rubbed her shoulder before getting beer from the fridge. The touching exchange both warmed Lexy, and sparked a wistful yearning deep inside that startled her.

How long had it been since she'd had a meaningful connection with a man? Too long, apparently. She hadn't even been dating lately. In her circle, the pool of desirable candidates was quite shallow. It hadn't helped that after seeing David exclusively for a year, he'd turned out to be an opportunist more interested in her last name than her.

Tanner pulled out a chair, the noise drawing her attention to him. He was watching her with the oddest expression. Not quite disapproval, but almost.

"Hey, how did Cody Lawson do?" Matt asked as he set down a bottle in front of Tanner. "He rode today, didn't he?"

"Yep, poor kid got his left spur caught in the rails the second they opened the chute. I thought he was nuts for hanging on. Turned out his hand got tangled in the rope. Baby Blue kept bucking. That son of a gun is one ornery bull. Nearly pulled the kid's arm out of its socket."

Shaking his head, Matt sat next to Rachel. "He take the reride?"

"Oh, yeah. Shouldn't have, though. His arm was bad."

"Hey," Matt said, shrugging. "We've all been there."

Lexy realized Matt was also involved with the rodeo. He looked to be late twenties and probably still on the pro tour.

"Hey, have you two eaten?" Rachel asked. "There's leftover meatloaf, mashed potatoes and green beans, and plenty of stuff for sandwiches."

Considering her impoverished circumstances, it would be sensible to accept the offer, but Lexy's hunger had passed and eating would mean drawing out the evening. What she needed was to be alone and regroup. This road trip seriously threw off her budget. But at least Oklahoma City was on the way, and hopefully her corporate credit card.

"I'm fine," she said at the same time Tanner said, "Lexy needs to eat."

"Thank you, Mr. Tanner, but I can speak for myself." She sent him a warning look, then turned back in time to see the amused curiosity in Matt's and Rachel's faces.

"So on top of feeling faint, you get grouchy when you don't eat. This is gonna be one hell of a long trip," Tanner muttered, then tipped the bottle to his lips.

"You're one to talk." It was a stupid, childish and completely unnecessary remark. She really did need more sleep. "Thank you so much for the tea. Very nice to meet you both, but if you don't mind—"

"Ms. Worthington tell you folks why she's here?" Tanner said, cutting her off, his gaze locked on her face. "Matt's the guy you want," he added, motioning with his chin. "Not me."

"For what?" Rachel spoke first, while Matt frowned.

Tanner smiled. "The name Gunderson ring a bell?"

Lexy hesitated. Obviously, it should. But she knew so little about the rodeo world. "I'm sorry," she said, giving Matt an apologetic look. "I don't know…"

"No reason you should." Matt grinned. With his blue eyes and sun-streaked hair, he was very good-looking and had a terrific smile. "Unless you're a rodeo fan and I'm guessing you aren't."

She didn't take offense at the skeptical way he eyed her clothes and hair. This was business and she was dressed appropriately. At least now she knew why Tanner had brought her here. He wanted her to leave him alone and go after Matt.

"This guy here is a three-time world champion bull rider," Tanner said. "And he ain't finished yet."

"Want to bet?" Rachel looped an arm through Matt's. "After this year, he's done."

"That true?"

Matt nodded. "I haven't kept it a secret."

Tanner sipped his beer, his expression thoughtful. "I heard rumors."

"Those weren't rumors," Rachel said. "He's going to raise rodeo stock here at the Lone Wolf."

Tanner looked as if he had more to say on the subject but he stayed quiet. Perhaps his thoughts mirrored hers. Did Rachel have something to do with Matt quitting?

"All right, I'll admit it," Rachel said, glancing between Tanner and Lexy. "I'm curious. What's going on between you two?"

"Oh, I'm going to make Mr. Tanner famous." Lexy made it a point to look at him and meet his deadpan expression. "We're on our way to a photo shoot in Houston."

He stared at her for another few seconds, shook his head, then drained his beer.

Lexy expected him to zing her but he didn't take the shot.

Rachel let out a laugh. "You can't stop there."

Matt didn't bother asking if Tanner wanted another beer. He cleared his throat, got up and brought him one.

Tanner nodded his thanks then eyed Lexy. "I thought you were leaving."

"I am." She got to her feet. "Thank you so much for the tea," she said to Rachel, smiled at Matt, then at Tanner. "Guess I'll see you tomorrow morning. Bright and early, I hope? And not too much beer, okay? We don't want you puffy for the camera."

His warning gaze dueled with hers and then he took a huge gulp.

"Wait. Is this about the calendar?" Rachel asked. "Do you know, um, what was her— Karina?"

"Yes." Well, Lexy hadn't seen that coming. "How do you know her? Was she here?"

Rachel nodded. "She was a guest at my family's dude ranch a few months back. She tried convincing my brothers and Matt into doing the calendar but, putting it kindly, they weren't interested." Rachel grinned at Matt. "See, you can still change your mind."

He muttered a mild oath and peered at Tanner. "You're doing it? That's a shock."

"He has no choice—he has a contract with my company," Lexy said absently, still thinking about Karina. She'd claimed to have made the rounds but Lexy assumed that meant Texas.

"I can speak for myself," he said, echoing her earlier words and aiming his gruff frown at her. Then he turned to Matt and Rachel. "I have a contract with her company."

They both laughed. Tanner didn't share their humor.

"Cheer up," Lexy told him. "The contract expires in ten days." She lightly patted his shoulder, and when he gave her a sharp look, his stubble grazed the back of her hand. She almost jumped out of her skin at the jolt of awareness shooting up her arm.

"Well, good night again."

"I thought you were staying in the guest room," Rachel said. "It's ready for you."

"Thanks, but I'd prefer to sleep in the trailer. On the couch," Lexy added. "Though I wouldn't turn down coffee in the morning."

Rachel looked as if she wanted to argue but sat back and smiled instead. As for Tanner, he wasn't smiling or talking. He was probably debating where to bury her body.

"YOU REALLY GONNA do that calendar?" Matt shook his head. "You're the last guy I'd expect to do something like that."

"Hell, no, I'm not gonna do it. You heard her...my contract expires soon. Even if I didn't drag my feet all the way to Houston, they can't make me resign."

"So that's why you stopped here. You're stalling."

Tanner shrugged. "That's not the only reason." He'd

wanted to talk to Matt, find out if the rumors about him getting out were true. A guy at the top of his game like Matt just didn't walk away. But Tanner didn't want to bring it up in front of Rachel. "This calendar crap," he said. "It doesn't make any sense since I'll be outta contract."

"I was thinking the same thing." Rachel stared off in the direction Lexy had disappeared. "She seemed surprised Karina had been here. Either they don't communicate well or this is some sort of competition between them."

Tanner sighed. "That would piss me off. Dragging me all the way to Houston to win a bet."

"Aren't you from Texas?" Matt asked. "You got family there, if I remember right."

"My grandparents live in West Texas. But that's a far cry from Houston."

"Why is she sleeping in the trailer?" Rachel asked, her mind obviously still on Lexy. "Does she think she's putting us out?"

"I don't know." Tanner snorted. "Probably thinks I'll drive off and leave her here."

Rachel laughed. "Would you?"

"Sure is a pleasant thought." Tanner smiled at Rachel's eye roll. He liked her. Matt was a lucky guy. "Don't let that gal fool you. Ms. Worthington can be a real pain in the ass."

"You just met her today?"

Tanner nodded, then said no to Matt's offer of another beer.

"You can't let her sleep out there," Rachel said, and he shrugged. "On the couch? And no bathroom. Really?"

"She can sleep wherever she wants." Not that he'd admit it, but he wasn't fond of the idea. The couch sucked. She'd be uncomfortable. "I can't make her do anything."

"I bet you can talk her into coming inside." Rachel tapped a finger on the table. "You said her name is Worthington. Any relation to The Worthington Group?"

"Yep, that's her family."

"Wow." Rachel slumped back. "I thought she looked familiar. I might've seen her picture in the Dallas newspaper when I was in college. The family is seriously rich... as in billions."

That rich? He thought Rachel might be wrong. "Then what's she doing here bothering me?"

"Good question." Rachel got up, grabbed her cell phone off the counter and brought it back to the table. Her fingers started moving and a minute later she said, "Alexis is immediate family, the only daughter of Marshall Worthington, but she doesn't seem to have an executive position with the company. Her brother is senior vice president."

"Yeah, I'm sure it has nothing to do with her winning personality," Tanner muttered like he didn't give a crap, but the snub bothered him. If that's what it was. Maybe she didn't want the responsibility. Either way, none of his concern.

"She sure seems down to earth. Look, if you won't go get her, then I will." Rachel waited for him to respond, and when he didn't she pushed away from the table.

"I'll go." Tanner slowly got to his feet, wincing at the pain slicing through his left thigh. "She's cranky enough without sleeping on an uncomfortable couch."

He didn't miss the sly smile Rachel gave Matt. If they thought he was hot for her and would let her talk him into the calendar, they were as nuts as Lexy.

6

TANNER OPENED THE door to the trailer, the old girl creaking loud enough to wake the dead. Though the noise hadn't disturbed Lexy. She lay curled up on the couch, her chin tucked to her chest, wearing the same clothes, minus the blazer, which hung over the back of a chair.

Man, she'd fallen asleep fast. It hadn't been more than ten minutes since she'd left them in the kitchen. The porch light shined in from the open window and he watched her face as he closed the door behind him. The racket should've been enough to make her open one eye. She didn't even move.

Her hair was loose, and longer and wavier than he'd pictured, draping her shoulder and hiding part of her face. He liked the wild, untamed look, though it made her look younger. Probably why she went with the ugly bun.

For a second he thought about leaving her alone. She was obviously exhausted. If she'd wanted to sleep in the guest room, she would've accepted Rachel's hospitality. Lexy didn't strike him as the demure type. But the woman didn't act like she came from billions, either.

He smiled at her small bare feet. Her toenails were painted blue. The same shade as her eyes. He cringed at the weird thought. Now, why would he remember the color of her eyes? They weren't green. He liked green-eyed women. Always had.

"Hey, Lexy."

Not so much as a twitch.

He flipped on the kitchen light and moved so it hit her directly in the face. "Alexis Worthington."

Her lashes fluttered and she turned her head, burrowing deeper, using her hair for cover.

Tanner touched her shoulder. "Rachel wants you inside."

She half whimpered, half growled, and he thought he might've heard a *no* somewhere in there. Then she shifted so that she faced the back of the couch. He wondered if she realized this new position made her butt stick out. Not that he was complaining. He leaned back for a better look. Nice view. Maybe he'd leave her right where she was.

Nah, he'd feel bad tomorrow. The couch was no place for her to sleep. She'd end up stiff as a board.

"Dammit, Lexy."

"Go away," she murmured, sounding groggy.

"Can't do that. I have orders." He waited for her to get up or say something. She did neither. "My shoulder is in bad enough shape," he said, sighing. "Don't make me carry you."

She flopped back to face him, struggling to shove the hair away from her eyes. "Oh, for God's sake. I'm sleeping. Can't you just—"

He caught her hand, and she let out a whoosh of minty breath as he pulled her to her feet. "Rachel has a room for you."

Her blouse hung open. Half her buttons were undone, exposing the lacy pink bra and smooth satiny skin. He hadn't meant to stare but she'd surprised him. She glanced down and pulled her blouse together.

"Sorry," he murmured, stuffing his hands into his pockets and switching his gaze to his boots.

"I must've fallen asleep before I finished changing...."

"I can step outside."

"No, that's okay." She got busy refastening the buttons. One of them ended up in the wrong hole but he doubted she'd appreciate him pointing that out. "What is it you wanted?" She raised her head, her eyes still unfocused with sleep. Without her shoes on she barely came up to his chin.

"I like your hair better down," he said, baffled that he'd spoken the words out loud.

"You woke me up to tell me that?"

"It makes no sense you sleeping out here. Come inside."

"I'm perfectly content on the couch." She lifted her nose in the air, and yeah, he could see a hint of that billionaire pedigree. "Or at least I was."

"So you don't care about not having a bathroom?"

"What are you talking about? There's one right there."

Tanner smiled. "Yep, and it works real well when the trailer's hooked up."

"What do you mean?" she asked, her gaze narrowing with suspicion. "You took a shower earlier."

"Where do you think the water and power comes from? You got a magic wand stuck someplace I don't know about?"

"Can't you plug this thing in somewhere?"

"Yeah, sure, princess, I'll get right on that." He grabbed her small bag, then glanced around. "Is this it?"

She nodded, noticed her shoes hiding under the couch and sat back down to reach them. "I wish you'd said something earlier."

"About?"

"The trailer being disabled."

From where he stood at the door, and with her leaning forward to slip on her shoes, he could see clear past her gaping neckline all the way to her belly. "You have to fix your blouse," he said and stared up at the ceiling.

"What? Oh. Hey, you wouldn't happen to have an extra T-shirt I could use. I'll replace it as soon as we get to Oklahoma City."

"My shirts are too big— Oklahoma City?" He watched her gracefully get to her feet. "I thought we were headed to Houston?"

"Well, OK City is on the way."

"No, it isn't."

"Neither is the Lone Wolf, yet here we are."

He waited while she searched the couch for something or another, then when she patted the back of her head, he figured it might be her hairpins. Wouldn't hurt his feelings none if she couldn't find them. She looked like a different person with her hair down. Kind of sexy, even with the conservative clothes and the faint black smudges under her eyes.

Her face had been too pale earlier but now there was a slight flush in her cheeks. And her lips sure were nice and plump. The kind that a man didn't want to stop kissing. He'd bet his gold buckle they were soft.

She stopped a couple feet away and frowned. "What's that expression for?"

"What?" He felt his own face get warm. "Nothing," he said gruffly and pushed past her to get to his dresser. "You want the shirt to sleep in?"

"That was the idea." She sighed. "Is it too weird to ask to borrow your clothes? I think so." She'd followed him and was standing so close he felt her breath on his arm. "Never mind. Forget it," she said, backing up. "I wasn't thinking."

"Now hold on." He caught her hand. "You weren't expecting a road trip. You're bound to run out of clothes."

She stared at their joined hands, and then met his eyes. "Tanner, I'm—" She drew in a quick breath. "You're very attractive and the next few days won't be easy…" She lowered her lashes and stared at his chest. "For me, anyway. But I won't let you use sex to wiggle out of your contract."

Tanner smiled. "Funny, I was thinking the same thing."

"I knew you'd try it." She looked disappointed.

"I'm not talking about me. I meant you." He let go when she yanked her hand away, blinking at him, confusion swirling in her eyes. "I figured you'd try to distract me and I'd end up in Houston before I knew what hit me."

"I would never use sex that way."

"Oh, hell, you know damn well you could get me going just by breathing."

They both froze, staring at each other with equal measures of distrust and awareness. He hadn't meant for that to slip out and he was pretty sure she knew it. Unfortunately, he was trapped between her and the bed. If anyone was going to make a move to leave and ease the tension, it would have to be Lexy.

She didn't seem to be in any hurry. Which could work out just fine, he thought, picturing the pretty pink lace bra she was wearing under the plain blouse. Bet he'd find a matching thong under her slacks. The hair was already down, and once the clothes came off, it wouldn't shock him to find a wild woman waiting to bust loose.

"No," she said, slowly shaking her head and taking a step back. "Uh-uh."

"I didn't say a word."

The farther she moved back, the better the view. Curvy hips, small waist, high, firm breasts. Those lips. "The librarian fantasy, right?"

He snorted, tried to keep his face a total blank. No way she'd guessed what he'd been thinking. "You want a shirt or not?"

"Not."

"Fine." He ducked into the bathroom and grabbed his shaving kit.

Lexy waited at the door, her small hand wrapped around the knob and the damnedest, most inappropriate image popped into his head. "Tanner?"

He sighed, almost afraid to meet her eyes. "What?"

"You won't leave without me tomorrow, will you?"

"Course not." He checked his pocket to make sure he had his phone in case Doug called. "I wouldn't do that to Matt and Rachel."

A wry smile lifted the corners of Lexy's mouth. "Look me in the eyes and tell me you won't leave me and I'll believe you."

He stopped right in front of her, lifted her hand off the doorknob and turned it over. "Here," he said, and dropped his truck keys on her palm. "Hold on to them if it makes you feel better."

She stared at the set of keys, then looked up at him. "I said I'd believe you."

"Hey, I'm just trying to let you rest easy. Give them back if you want."

With a small smile, she closed her fist around them and stuffed the keys in her pocket. "This is really nice of you."

"Nice has nothing to do with it. I don't want you tired and cranky the whole drive tomorrow."

"Of course."

"You gonna open the door? Or stand there with that silly grin on your face?"

She stretched up on tiptoes and lightly kissed his cheek. "Thank you."

Shit. A kiss on the cheek like he was her grandfather? Why not just put him out to pasture already.

He touched her hair, rubbed the silky strands between his thumb and forefinger. "Wait," he said, mesmerized by her lips. He had to feel them for himself, find out if they were as soft as they looked. Show her he wasn't over the hill yet.

Man, he was just looking for trouble. He knew it sure as she was standing there. So why wasn't he backing off? It wasn't too late.

She watched with darkened eyes as he lowered his head. He ran a hand down her arm and had barely brushed his mouth across hers when she drew back. "Tanner..."

"Just a kiss, that's it," he murmured, pulling her closer, but ready to release her at the first sign of resistance.

Placing a hand on his chest, she leaned into him. "Just a kiss, nothing more, right?" she whispered, the sweet caress of her warm breath on his chin enough to make him promise her anything.

If that wasn't warning enough, her clean feminine scent confirmed he was asking for trouble. "Nothing more," he agreed, moving his hand to her lower back. "Unless you ask for it."

Her quiet throaty laugh made his body tighten. "I do like a confident man," she said, tipping her head back and offering up her lips.

He settled his mouth on hers, gently applying pressure, then teased her lips apart. She slid her palm up his chest and looped her arm around his neck. Her breasts felt full and soft pressed against him, like honest-to-goodness real breasts. Nothing fake about them.

She tasted sweet and willing, satisfaction warming him when she cupped the back of his neck and pulled his mouth closer. Her lips were every bit as soft as they looked, and eager, too. But it was the low, sexy moan that almost made him scoop her up in his arms and carry her to his bed.

With a breathy gasp, she moved her head back. "We agreed on one kiss."

"I know. We haven't finished." Tanner saw the fire burning in her eyes. He almost smiled. Purity Club. Like hell. "Don't penalize me for liking 'em long, slow and deep."

On another soft gasp her lips parted again.

Lowering his head, he brushed her mouth with his, and she wasn't saying no. He slid his hand down her back, his calloused thumb snagging on her fine silk blouse.

He stopped.

She hadn't seemed to notice but it sure bothered him.

He released her, and moved away from her tempting mouth. "Let's go," he said, ignoring her startled expression. "Rachel wants to show you to your room."

It took Lexy a minute after she'd awoken to remember she was in Matt and Rachel's guest room. Another ten seconds to admit to herself that Will Tanner scared her. He was a damn good kisser and that was arguably her biggest weakness. Right behind hazelnut gelato.

She kicked free of the gray sheets and rolled to the edge of the queen bed. Hoping the nightstand clock was wrong, she grabbed her watch. No, it really was after nine. So much for hitting the road by eight.

Sighing, she put on yesterday's blouse, picked up her overnight bag, then peeked outside her door. The hall was empty. Muffled voices carried up from the first floor. So did the tempting aroma of coffee and bacon. The door to the bathroom she was sharing with Tanner was open, so she made a dash.

The water heated quickly and the shower spray was perfect. She'd be in total heaven if only her stubborn thoughts would move beyond last night's kiss. She hoped it hadn't been a mistake. Shame on her if she let the momentary lapse interfere with her getting him to Houston on time. Normally men didn't intimidate her, sexually or otherwise. But something about that damn cowboy made her edgy.

Maybe it was the simple fact that he was so different from the guys she knew. Even the dark, brooding ones who'd thrilled her as a teenager. But she'd grown tired of them, just as she had the corporate crowd with their foreign sports cars and expensive hobbies.

Or maybe it wasn't nerves at all. Just hunger. How could she still smell bacon in the shower? Rachel would offer breakfast and this time Lexy would eat. Screw her pride. She'd send them flowers and a wine basket once she got to Oklahoma City.

She shampooed her hair knowing she'd have to let it air dry, which was never a pretty sight. It didn't matter. She'd pull it back later. Deciding on what to wear wasn't a problem. She'd brought one pair of slacks, jeans and two blouses, never dreaming she'd be gone more than a couple days.

After applying some mascara, she stuffed everything back into her bag, tidied up behind her and hurried downstairs. From the clang of pots, she knew someone was in the kitchen but she crossed the foyer to leave her bag near the front door. When she heard Tanner's voice, she stopped and looked around. The sound of Matt's laughter drew her attention to the den.

"I'm serious." It was Tanner again. "You'd look mighty good on a calendar."

Matt succinctly told him what he could do to himself.

Tanner chuckled. "Remember that bar in Jacksonville with the mechanical bull in the back room? That tall blonde pulled her top right off in full view of everyone so you could sign her breasts."

"I was pretty drunk, but yeah, I remember. I shouldn't have ridden that day. My ribs weren't healed yet. They felt like they were on fire."

"Yep, I did the same thing in Louisiana three months later. You were there, too. Duke and Cardona bitched like little girls when you showed up. Duke had been eyeing this pretty brunette but they knew all they'd get were your leftovers."

Matt groaned. "Rachel hears you and I'll kick your ass."

Lexy glanced over her shoulder toward the kitchen. She'd prefer Rachel didn't catch her eavesdropping, either.

"Come on…she's gotta know how it is on the tour," Tanner said. "Anyway, you weren't with her back then."

"I'm not worried she'd be jealous. That woman would tease me until my dying day."

Tanner laughed. "Better prepare her. If you retire, there'll be a million women wailing in the streets."

"No *if* about it. Three more events and I'm done." After a long pause that had Lexy considering whether it was time for her to move on, Matt said, "You're not here about the calendar or to discuss old times. What's up with you?"

Tanner's sigh was heartfelt. "I think I blew it. I should've left the tour when I had the chance."

"Had the chance? It's your call. You quit when you want. Don't let the media influence you."

"Gotta hand it to you, Gunderson. You're smart. Leaving while you're still young and on top."

"You know what the average age of a bull rider is? I think it's around twenty-six now. I'm twenty-nine. Smart would've been to stop a few years and five injuries ago."

"But you were still racking up titles."

"Could've gone the other way," Matt said. "The truth is, I only wanted out because of Nikki and then Rachel. Smart had nothing to do with it."

"How is your sister? I thought Nikki was living here with you."

"She is, off and on. She's tight with Rachel's brother and they've started fixing up an old ranch house not far from here. Montana's been good for her. She's happy." Matt paused again. "You, though, don't look so hot."

"I haven't ranked in the top ten for two years and it's costing me more to stick around than I'm earning."

"It's a no-brainer, then. Stop."

"Man, not on a losing streak."

"Seriously?" Matt scoffed. "That's when you get out, buy a ranch, make a living at something that won't land you in the hospital every six months. Is money an issue?"

"I've socked away enough. I'm sure you noticed last night that I've still got Betsy."

"Yeah, good for you for not blowing everything on booze and new gadgets, but that trailer belongs in a museum already."

"She gets me where I'm going." Tanner's indignant tone made Lexy smile.

"So, maybe you should do the calendar thing."

"Hell, no. Just what I need, go out a loser and be the laughingstock of the rodeo association."

Lexy stiffened, and did everything in her power not to butt in. Though if she wanted to learn if sabotaging their trip was on the agenda she was better off staying hidden. No, she wouldn't jump to conclusions. He hadn't said he'd miss the photo shoot, he just wouldn't do the calendar.

"You have a contract. Be careful how you play this out. They could sue."

"So I've heard." Tanner's palpable disgust pricked her guilty conscience. But then he added, "Don't worry, I know just how to handle Lexy Worthington."

The words hurt.

Why? Because they'd kissed? So what? No reason for her to be touchy. She turned for the kitchen as hurt slid to anger. *All right, buddy,* she thought. *Game on.*

7

"YOU WANT ME to pull off at the next exit?" Tanner glanced over at her. She'd been texting or doing whatever she did on that fancy phone of hers for the past hour. "There's a travel stop with clean restrooms and a big convenience store."

"How do you know they're clean?" she asked without looking up.

"What kind of question is that?"

"I've been with you for the past twenty-four hours and we haven't been anywhere near Billings until now. I'm just wondering how you can be so sure the bathrooms are clean."

He should've known better than to try and be nice. She'd been cranky since they'd left the Lone Wolf four hours ago. "I met the retired couple who bought the place last year. They keep it in tip-top shape."

"Oh, so you're merely speculating."

"What's your problem? I figured with all that bacon and eggs in your belly you'd be more agreeable today."

She sent him a sidelong glare. "I wasn't a pig, if that's what you're implying. I ate what Rachel served me."

"What, then? You mad about the kiss?"

She went back to her phone, her wavy hair falling forward and hiding her face. "What kiss?"

Tanner smiled at her snooty tone. She could pretend she'd forgotten about it if that made her feel better. Though he had a feeling she might've revisited those few moments when she'd let her guard down. Just as he'd done while lying in bed last night, staring into the dark and wondering if she was sleeping naked.

She sure was an interesting woman. Certainly not easy to figure out, which was always refreshing. Man, he wouldn't mind more of that kissing. But he wasn't getting his hopes up. She wouldn't be happy with their next overnight stop.

His thoughts kept going back to what he'd learned from Rachel about the Worthingtons being crazy loaded. Certain ladies had a weakness for rodeo cowboys and he'd been with his share of them from bleached-blonde cocktail waitresses to southern socialites sporting diamonds the size of Alabama. He knew what rich women smelled and tasted like, how they looked, how they sounded, and Lexy just didn't quite fit the mold. Sure, she wore expensive clothes and that gold watch must've set her back a chunk. And occasionally she did that haughty lift of her chin. But mostly she seemed too…normal.

Course her family was in the billionaire category and he doubted he'd hobnobbed with anyone that rich. Factoring in that she came from old money, which he'd discovered made a difference in how people behaved, could account for her not being the spoiled type who expected people to jump through hoops.

"Help me out with something," he said, taking his eyes off the highway to glance at her. At least she'd put the phone down. "You being so rich and all, I don't understand why you'd come get me yourself."

"First of all, I'm not rich," she said, this time sounding as if she'd been giving servants orders her whole life. "Secondly—okay, why are you smiling like that?"

"Rachel filled me in on your family." He eased his foot

off the accelerator, knowing the area was a speed trap for the next five-mile stretch. "By the way, you're right. That internet is a goldmine. I'll have to do some poking around."

Lexy sighed, and he did all he could not to laugh. He wasn't as ignorant of the online phenomenon as he'd let on. Sometimes he read news off the other riders' iPads. But it never occurred to him to use a computer to look up information or buy an iPad for himself. Or to spend half his waking hours glued to a screen, giving folks a play-by-play of his life.

"So…did she look up The Worthington Group?" she asked casually. "Or my family?" She shrugged a shoulder. "Or me?"

Well, wasn't that interesting? Lexy was worried. It was in her voice, in the way she'd shifted positions so she could watch him without turning her head. She'd be kicking herself if she knew how much curiosity she'd just stirred up. Obviously, there was something she didn't want him finding out about her.

"I don't know," he said evenly. "I guess the company."

She seemed to relax. "Yes, my family is rich. I'm not."

Damn, he'd have to find someone with one of those iPads. He had a good idea where. "Hard to believe some of those millions haven't trickled down," he said, deliberately eyeing her gold Rolex. "Unless you pissed off mommy and daddy."

"Are you always this rude and nosy?"

"Only when I'm bored because I can't listen to my own damn radio."

She had the grace to blush. They had opposing opinions regarding country music, and he'd given in until they caught a station they could agree on.

Without a fuss, she reached over and turned on the radio. "There."

He turned it off again. "You haven't answered. Why are you here?"

"We covered that yesterday," she said irritably, then catching herself, more sweetly added, "You're important to us. We think you'd be a wonderful spokesperson."

"Knock it off." He didn't buy it for a minute and not just because she'd been acting as if she'd like to leave him hog-tied on the side of the road. "Word of advice. Don't go into politics."

"Career advice coming from you... Now that's rich."

Her words stung even though he knew she'd meant nothing more than to annoy him. Or could be she considered him a dumb cowboy who made a living getting bucked off broncs because he had no other skill. She wouldn't be entirely wrong. "I don't have to be the sharpest knife in the drawer to know you stink at tact."

"I'm sorry," she said. "Truly, I am. That was an unforgivably boorish thing for me to say."

Tanner laughed. "Boorish. Okay."

"I'm trying to apologize."

"Apology accepted."

"I think that's you," Lexy said at the same time he realized his phone was ringing in his pocket.

He hated seeing people talking and driving but he whipped the cell phone out in case it was his brother. Sure enough. "Hey, Doug." Tanner spotted a rest-stop sign up ahead. This wasn't a conversation he wanted to have within earshot of Lexy. "Call me back in three minutes."

"But I have reservations—"

"Three minutes," Tanner repeated and disconnected before he got too steamed. Reservations. He doubted it had taken Doug a whole day to pick up his messages.

"What happens in three minutes?" Lexy asked.

He almost missed the exit, signaled at the last second and steered the truck toward the red-brick building. It wasn't much as far as rest stops went; bathrooms, a few vending machines and stacks of tourist brochures, if he remembered correctly. Though all he needed was privacy.

"I'm gonna take this call," he said, pulling into the first parking stall. "You can wait in the truck or go use the facilities." Out of habit he picked up his Stetson, settled it on his head and then grabbed the key from the ignition.

Lexy didn't answer. He left her and started toward the picnic tables grouped at the edge of the woods, knowing to avoid the one sitting under a cottonwood. Too many splinters. No telling how many times he'd traveled this route headed from one rodeo to the next. It wasn't a bad life. Not for a single guy. If he'd had a wife and kids he suspected he would've switched to ranching by now. Some of the married cowboys balanced travel and family just fine. But he knew if he ever got hitched he'd want to be home every night. No way he'd be a part-time father like his useless old man.

Doug called as Tanner passed the first table, occupied by a young woman and two small children fighting over sandwiches. "Where are you? What's that noise?"

"At a rest stop." The connection wasn't great so Tanner kept walking until the kids' squawking faded. He was still pissed at how long it'd taken Doug to call but he kept his cool, told himself Doug had probably waited for Helen to fax him a copy of the contract. "Tell me I have an out."

"Wish I could."

Tanner stared off toward his truck. Lexy had gotten out and was headed for the building. "My deal was with Sundowner, not The Worthington Group."

"No, not true."

"What the hell, bro? We only discussed the Sundowner."

Doug hesitated, and it finally dawned on Tanner that his brother had been fresh out of law school when he'd negotiated the contract. It was likely that he'd made a mistake. If that were so, no sense rubbing it in.

"Look, what's done is done," Tanner said, leaning against the trunk of a cottonwood. "But any chance there's a loophole?" He didn't know why he was grasping at straws. At this point he knew someone like Lexy wouldn't waste her time coming this far if she thought it could wind up a dead end.

"Afraid not. We're talking The Worthington Group here. Their legal team doesn't allow for loopholes." Doug sighed. "I didn't hang you out to dry. Two years ago you were barely making it to the finals. Your winnings had gone down considerably. A third sponsor was about to drop you. The writing was on the wall and I figured it wouldn't hurt for you to pick up some extra cash."

Tanner's whole body tensed. Everything his brother said was true, none of it news, but hearing it out loud? Man, it felt like a kick to the groin. "You still should've made it clear who I was climbing into bed with and let me make the call."

"Frankly, I didn't think it mattered. The Sundowner didn't fit Worthington's profile. I think the CEO's son was trying to make his mark with the new line. Of course you know the brand tanked." Doug snorted. "Now you say they're looking into men's fragrances? That doesn't make sense, either."

Tanner saw Lexy leave the building. She'd surprised him when she showed up for breakfast in jeans. She looked real good in them. "You know anything about the daughter? Alexis Worthington. Did she have anything to do with Sundowner?"

"No idea. Why?"

"Anything you find out about her, let me know."

"Is this fragrance line her baby? You might want to think about renewing your contract in case it's a success."

"Jesus, how did you get through law school without a brain in that head?" Tanner watched Lexy approach the truck. The snug jeans and that nice round backside weren't the only reasons he wasn't so irritated about this little detour anymore. She was interesting, a real puzzle. That she knew how to kiss didn't hurt, either.

"Why the curiosity about her?"

"Because she's the one escorting me to Houston."

Doug paused. "Bullshit."

"They usually do." He pushed off the tree and headed for the truck.

"But that doesn't— You're sure she's Alexis Worthington?"

"I saw her driver's license."

"Why would she personally be handling you?"

"Hey, bro, I forgot you have reservations," Tanner said with as much phony sympathy as he could muster. "Didn't mean to keep you." He smiled when his brother yelled, "Wait!" right before Tanner disconnected the call.

Yeah, maybe he was being a jerk. He knew Doug had acted out of concern when he'd negotiated the contract. The last thing he would've wanted to do was remind Tanner that his career was circling the drain. But that didn't excuse what he'd done.

Though to be fair, he knew some of his annoyance went deeper than Doug making a wrong call. Tanner had just turned fourteen when their mom died half a world away. Doug had been a rowdy eight-year-old. With their father drifting in and out of their lives, Tanner had taken the big brother role seriously. Even though they'd lived with Nana and Pop, Tanner learned how to do laundry, fry eggs and pack lunches. When Doug had scraped his knee, it was Tanner who'd slapped a Band-Aid on it. And when the time came for college and law school, he'd covered Doug's tuition.

Now it seemed the tables had turned. Doug was worrying about Tanner's future and making decisions for him, and he didn't like it.

Lexy was already in her seat, strapped in, waiting for him when he opened the driver's door. She'd pulled her hair back, which was a real shame. The upside was that he could see her face better, from the cute ski-slope nose to her small, stubborn chin. Unhappy as he was with Doug's lapse in judgment, Tanner had to admit, he wasn't minding this little trip with Lexy.

"Everything okay?" she asked.

"Right as rain." He removed his Stetson and set it on the console between them. "How about you?"

She let out a sigh, looking as if she'd rather be sitting in a dentist chair. "Think of any more clean bathrooms along the way, let me know."

Two HOURS AND two stops later, tired of the dry prairies of southern Montana, Lexy closed her eyes and laid her head back against the seat. The sky was clear and brilliantly blue, and she'd seen a few green mountain ranges but they seemed puny after the Rockies. She definitely preferred the northwestern part of the state and thought of the picture taped to Tanner's fridge. It wouldn't surprise her if he'd taken the photo somewhere near Blackfoot Falls.

Opening her eyes, about to ask him, she saw him use his signal. She hoped he only meant to change lanes, but no, he steered the truck toward the exit.

"We can't possibly need gas again." Lexy checked her watch. She knew nothing about towing a large trailer but she did know they were making horrible time.

"Nope. We still have half a tank."

"Then why are we stopping?"

"You'll like the park here. There's even a nice motel across the street, and next to it, The Cowboy Café serves a rib-eye steak that'll make your mouth water for days."

She stared at his profile, unable to tell if he was teasing. "You want to stop for the night?"

"Don't worry, they have room," he said. "I called and reserved a spot."

"No." She shook her head. "Absolutely not. We got a late start and we have over four hours of daylight left. We have to keep driving."

"And whose fault was it that we got a late start, princess?"

"Sure, keep calling me that," she said, glaring. "That won't make me want to strangle you in your sleep." They passed a poster board stuck to a post, and she twisted around when she thought she saw the words *festival* and *rodeo*. "What did that sign say?"

"What sign?" He didn't even try to hide his smirk.

"Oh, God." She wanted to scream. "What are we doing here?"

"I already told you. Bunking down for the night."

"So you don't know anything about a rodeo?"

"Course I do. It's been a Carterville tradition for fifteen years running."

Lexy took a deep breath, ordered herself to stay calm. After all, she'd already known stalling was part of his plan. "Will you be riding?"

He frowned at her. "This is an amateur event."

"Oh. So there's no particular reason to stay here."

"There's plenty reason. I like the trailer park and I'm too tired to do any more driving."

"I could take over."

He waited until he'd cleared the intersection and turned left. "You ever towed a trailer before?"

"No, but I'm willing to give it a try."

"Not with Betsy you won't. I don't let just anyone tow her, much less a rookie."

Lexy hated being held hostage. Short on money and

clout, that's exactly how she felt. "You should be jumping at the chance I could demolish that old tin can. My insurance would hand you a fat check."

"That's the trouble with you rich people. You think money fixes everything." Something apparently had caught his eye. He slowed the truck, craning his neck as they passed a string of storefronts.

"I choose to take the high ground and ignore what you just said." She turned in her seat to follow his gaze, although she had no idea what he was looking at. "How would you like it if I made a sweeping generalization about cowboys?"

"So much for taking the high ground." He made a sharp right turn that had her clutching the armrest.

"You're going to make me carsick."

"Don't mess up my upholstery."

"Ah, your concern is touching," she said, relieved that he coasted to the stop sign. She hadn't lied. Motion sickness had been a problem since she was a kid. He made another right but less jerky. "Are we circling?"

"I have to check out something."

"What?"

"It'll only take a minute." Driving at a snail's pace, he squinted at a sixties-style, rusting blue van parked in front of a bar called Flying High. His gaze swept the sidewalk, then returned to the van.

"Someone you know?"

"Maybe."

Judging by the firm set of his mouth, Tanner didn't like whoever owned the vehicle. After a final look out of the side mirror he picked up speed. His pensive mood made her more curious, but she left him to his thoughts while she checked out the shops with their Western-themed window displays and colorful banners welcoming guests to the annual festival.

Someone had gone overboard with signs, offering everything from pony rides to shooting competitions. There were pie-eating contests and games she'd never heard of, and the local 4H Club would be auctioning cows and pigs the kids had raised for their projects. And of course the rodeo, the centerpiece of the four-day celebration.

In minutes they made it to the other side of town, where Lexy spotted the trailer park. It was ridiculously crowded. Maybe she'd get lucky and find that Tanner had been bluffing about reserving a space. He sure wouldn't get one now.

"Is this it?" she asked, watching him survey the rows of trailers and motor coaches.

He didn't seem concerned. "Yep, and there's the motel."

The one-story pink building across the street was a complete eyesore. On the upside, the room rate had to be rock-bottom. Just like her finances.

"I know it's not much, but I can guarantee you it's clean."

"Ever stay there?"

"Nope. Betsy goes with me everywhere I go."

"Of course she does," Lexy muttered. If they'd flown to Houston yesterday, he would now be someone else's problem and she'd be back home. Mission accomplished in record time.

"No need for sarcasm," he said, grinning at her. "Though I understand why you might be a little jealous."

She rolled her eyes and stared bleakly at the pink building. In front of each room was a parking stall and every one was taken. No vacancy would be fine with her. She'd rather sleep on his couch and not have to worry her credit card would be declined.

Tanner pulled the truck along the curb in front of the office. "I'll let you off here so you can check in while I get squared away across the street."

"Are you that sure you have a spot?"

"Positive."

Hesitating, she rested her hand on the door handle. "The motel looks full. I may be out of luck."

"Won't know till you try."

"Right," she murmured. "What if— Never mind."

"Well now, Alexis." He slid an arm along the seat behind her shoulders and leaned close enough to kiss her. "If I didn't know better, I'd think you wanted an invitation to share my bed."

"In your dreams." She opened the door and hopped out. He was still grinning when she hurried to the office.

A balding man sat behind the counter, chuckling at something on a small TV. He reluctantly glanced up at the sound of the overhead bell triggered by the door. A woman wearing a green muumuu emerged from a back room, and his attention returned to the screen.

"Oh, no, Henry, don't trouble yourself none," she said with a long-suffering roll of her eyes, which he completely disregarded.

"You looking for a room?" She sized Lexy up, starting with her gold hoop earrings and then leaning over the counter to look at her jeans and bronze leather sandals.

"Yes," Lexy said, taken aback by the woman's lack of manners. "I don't have a reservation and I realize it's last minute—"

"No problem. Got a man with you?"

"Pardon me?"

The woman squinted out the window. "You here alone or have you got company?"

"I'm alone."

"I had to ask. We charge more for double occupancy."

"So you do have a room…" Suppressing her disappointment, she got out her wallet.

"We weren't sure we'd rent it since Henry is still working on the plumbing problem. But you seem like a nice young woman and it wouldn't be right turning you away."

She grinned, and Lexy tried her best to ignore the red lipstick smear on her teeth.

"Plumbing problem?"

"The sink's hot water faucet is kinda hit and miss, if you
know what I mean." Her gaze went to the gold card Lexy
laid on the counter. "Honey, we don't take that one. The
percentage that company charges us poor small business
owners is akin to highway robbery."

Her husband looked over, straining to see the card.
"Them people are crooks."

"We take that one there," the woman said, pointing to
the VISA in Lexy's open wallet.

The account was too close to its credit limit for Lexy's
peace of mind. "This is my company card, and since I'm
here on business," she said, sliding the gold card back toward the woman, "I really need to use this one. How about
you tack on, say, ten percent—" She smiled. The room
couldn't be more than forty dollars. An extra four wouldn't
break her since she had a hundred dollars to spare.

"Nope." She folded her thick arms. "Comes a time in a
person's life when they gotta be willing to stand on prin-
ciple."

"I don't suppose that could come at another time?"
Lexy asked, her hopes crumbling under the woman's glare.
"Right." She cleared her throat and pulled out the VISA.
Maybe…just maybe, she'd be able to squeeze in another
small charge. "How much is it for a night?"

"One hundred and fifty dollars."

8

LEXY'S BREATH CAUGHT. "Would you repeat that, please?"

The woman had already picked up the VISA. "I know we could get more during a busy week like this, but we aren't greedy people. Right, Henry?"

"That's right, Vivian."

"Wait," Lexy said, stopping the woman from processing the card. It wouldn't be approved at that amount. "You're serious. You're asking for a hundred and fifty dollars for a room *here*...with plumbing problems."

Vivian shrugged. "Otherwise it would've been a hundred and seventy-five."

"Don't forget to add the tax," Henry said without turning from the TV.

Lexy stared in horror as the woman poised the card to be swiped. "No, don't—" It was too late. Vivian had run the VISA through the system.

With nothing to do but wait, embarrassment burning in her cheeks, Lexy watched the woman's expression darken as she read the small screen on the processing device.

"Your card's been declined."

"I know," Lexy said, putting out her hand. "My account isn't past due, just close to my credit limit." Why had she felt compelled to explain? Henry and Vivian had some nerve accusing anyone of robbery. A hundred and fifty for one of their rooms? It was absurd. "My card, please."

"No can do. The company wants me to confiscate it."

"That's not possible."

"Says it right here. Look for yourself." She swiveled the device around for Lexy to see.

"Oh, great. Just great. Look, I'm begging you. Try this other card. Add a twenty—" She stopped. A two-hundred-dollar charge would push her over the limit. "How about if I give you my watch for collateral? Tomorrow I'll have cash wired to your bank."

She hadn't wanted to involve Norma, but at this point she was desperate. Lexy pulled off the gold Rolex and offered it to Vivian, who took it with suspicious reluctance.

"I gotta admit," she said, turning it over. "It's a good knockoff. Better than the one I almost bought in Vegas."

Lexy sighed. "It's not a knockoff. Look." She indicated the trademark crown located on the clasp, right where it was supposed to be.

Henry got up and walked over to them. "I'll handle this," he told Vivian. "I'm sure you have something else to do."

The woman frowned. They exchanged a look, then she disappeared into the back room.

He held the watch in his palm as if gauging its weight, then brought it up for a closer inspection.

Lexy was starting to regret the offer. She'd only meant for them to keep it until Norma wired money. But what if they refused to return it? Naturally, she'd ask for a receipt, but this was a small town. They probably knew everyone here, including law enforcement, and she'd be out of luck trying to get the watch back. That would be awful. Unbearable. She'd be better off asking Tanner to let her sleep in his trailer.

He'd give her untold grief, delight in accusing her of wanting to get in his jeans. God. She could hear it all now.

He'd tease her mercilessly. But she could swallow whatever he dished out. Better than losing the watch Gramms had given her a week before she'd passed away. Lexy had been forced to pawn it once before and it made her sick. She'd ended up reclaiming it early, which had set her even further back financially.

Dammit, she needed to be back in her father's good graces more than she needed her pride. Tanner could do his worst…so what. Though there was another solution. She'd have to lie her butt off, but only to Tanner, and somehow that didn't seem to count as much in her mind. All she had to do was tell him she'd lost her credit cards at one of the stops they'd made. He'd either offer her a loan or his couch. Simple. She should've thought of it earlier.

"It's okay," Lexy said. "I don't need a room after all." Let them find another poor sucker willing to overlook their price gouging. She put out her hand. "I'll have my watch back, please."

Vivian returned from the back room and exchanged another enigmatic look with her husband.

"My watch?" Lexy repeated, growing apprehensive when they ignored her outstretched hand. "I want my damn watch."

"No need to cuss," Vivian said. "Or we'll be forced to call the sheriff."

"Sounds like a great idea to me."

Behind her she heard the door open. Male laughter drowned out the overhead bell. She turned slightly, dismayed to find Tanner entering the office…talking to a man wearing a tan sheriff's uniform.

"Am I glad to see you, Craig," Vivian said, her pitch dialed up to melodramatic. "This is the woman I called you about."

"Lexy?" Tanner frowned. "What's going on?"

She froze, unable to think fast enough. Much as she

didn't want him privy to her awkward situation, she needed him on her side.

"Thought you said you didn't have a man." Vivian snorted. "Lied about that, too, I see."

"I didn't lie. Tanner isn't with me. I mean, he is, but not that way."

"Tanner?" Henry narrowed his gaze. "Will Tanner?"

"Yep." He glanced at the older man, then quickly brought his confused gaze back to Lexy.

"Hold it, Pop," the sheriff said, putting up a hand to Henry. "One thing at a time."

Perfect. Just perfect. Henry was the sheriff's father.

"I saw you ride in Colorado Springs several years back," Henry said, ignoring his son. "Shoulda seen all those dropped jaws when you stayed on four extra seconds. You were really something in your day."

Tanner flinched.

Lexy doubted anyone else had noticed the slight jerk or the light that seemed to die in his eyes. Her thoughts shot back to the conversation with Matt that she'd overheard. Stepping aside for younger, more skilled riders had to be rough, even worse because it was so wretchedly public.

Henry came around the counter. "Sure would like to shake your hand, son."

Tanner handled the situation with grace but the tightness around his mouth tugged at Lexy's heart. "Craig said you were a rodeo fan. I pass through now and again and meant to stop in."

"No worries. Me and the missus have been doing some traveling while we can still get around." Henry glanced at his wife, then at Lexy. "So you know her."

"I do." Tanner met her eyes, his mouth curving in a faint smile. "She been giving you trouble?"

Glaring, she jabbed a forefinger at him. "Don't start. I'm not in the mood."

The sheriff laughed. "Can I get back to work without you making any more nuisance calls?" he asked, his query directed at Vivian.

She sniffed. "I wish you were more like your brother. Kevin wouldn't think of sassing me."

Lexy tensed. Why did parents do that comparison crap?

Craig heaved a tired sigh, then touched the brim of his tan Stetson. "Sorry for the misunderstanding, ma'am," he said to Lexy. "Hope you enjoy the festival."

She smiled, not bothering to correct him. They weren't here for fun and if she could convince Tanner to get back on the road, she would. Right now, though, all she wanted was for her watch to be returned.

As if reading her mind, the sheriff nodded to Vivian. "Give her the watch."

She started to pass it over, then made a final inspection. "This look real to you?"

"Mom."

"All right." Vivian dropped the watch in Lexy's hand. "You still need the room?"

Lexy blinked, then glanced at Tanner. "Do I?" At any other time his shocked expression would've made her laugh. "I'm asking if we're staying in town overnight."

"Ah." He gave her a crooked grin. "Yep, we are."

The sheriff stopped at the door. "I'm on duty until nine but I'll likely run into you later."

Tanner nodded. "Any chance you've seen J.D.?"

"He's not here. You probably saw his van, though."

"What?" Disdain altered Tanner's features. "He finally lose it at poker?"

"Not from what I heard. He won a Caddy off some fella who ran out of money. Been on a winning streak for over a week now." Craig's radio crackled and he bent his ear toward it. "Gotta go," he said. "See you later."

"We still haven't settled on how you're paying for the room," Vivian said, her tone snippy.

God, Lexy hated this. The story she'd concocted about losing her cards wouldn't work anymore. "What if Tanner vouches for me?"

Vivian's sigh ended with a nod.

"Remember that year you rode in Fort Worth and it was televised…" Henry had latched on to Tanner again, even though it was obvious he seemed distracted.

Lexy wanted to be done with this humiliating situation then left alone to lick her wounds. Before she could say anything, Tanner dug out a wad of cash from his jeans' pocket and peeled off a pair of hundred-dollar bills.

Henry returned one of them, plus a couple twenties. Apparently, he wasn't willing to gouge his rodeo hero. Then the man continued talking nonstop until she and Tanner were out the door.

"Thanks," Lexy murmured, fisting the key to room 112 and keeping her head down until they were outside. Her face was still warm from embarrassment, and it wasn't over. She couldn't imagine what he was thinking. "I'll pay you back tomorrow. The day after at the latest."

"Don't worry about it," he said absently. "Your bag is in the truck. We should get it before you go to your room."

She hesitated, then nodded. As much as she wanted to disappear, she doubted she'd feel any better later.

He wasn't in a chatty mood and that was fine with her. They crossed the busy street to the trailer park, stopped several times by people who recognized Tanner. He was pleasant to everyone, and while she was ready to scream, the interruptions seemed to pull him out of his preoccupation.

The trailer was parked under the shade of a huge aspen, but not the truck. An unseasonably hot sun beat down on the cab, and she really hoped her makeup hadn't completely melted by now.

Tanner used the remote to unlock the door and pulled it open. He started to reach inside for the bag, then backed up, empty-handed, and frowned at her. "What happened back there? You can't be traveling without a credit card or money."

Lexy sighed. "They wouldn't take my corporate card because they won't do business with that company. Then there was a mix-up with my VISA. And I didn't bring enough cash with me. Stupid, I know."

A lazy smirk lifted the corners of his mouth. And then he really annoyed her by not saying anything. Not a word. Did he know she was lying?

"I'll pay you back," she said when he reached inside for her bag. Her gaze fell to his backside. The worn denim molded him perfectly.

"Damn right you'll pay me back," he said, bringing out her bag and closing the door. "With all the money your company makes…"

"So now you're an expert on The Worthington Group?"

"I know enough to bring money with me when I travel." He ran a gaze down her front, his expression brimming with amusement. "I didn't figure you for being in the bartering business."

"You're hilarious. Give me my bag."

"Guess your poor financial standing means I have to buy you dinner, too."

"That won't be necessary." She tried to grab the handle but he pulled the bag out of reach.

"Hold on now. I'm walking you back to your room."

"That's ridiculous."

He ignored her and started toward the street. "Think you'll be ready to eat in an hour?"

She had to hurry to keep up with his longer strides. "I'm not hungry. You seem to know people around here. Eat with them. Don't feel as if you have to entertain me."

"Hell, you should be entertaining me. Dragging me all the way to Houston," he muttered irritably, though she knew he wasn't really mad. "You should pay for gas, too. I'll put that on your tab."

"Absolutely. Please do."

He stopped to let the cars pass, then took her elbow as they stepped onto the asphalt.

Wondering what he was up to, she turned to look at him.

"I was gonna put my arm around you," he said, leaning close and speaking low. "But I wasn't sure where this elbow would land."

Lexy didn't want to laugh. She'd just been humiliated, and to make matters worse, Tanner was being a gentleman about it. But the truth was, she was hot and tired. Besides, this was the old Tanner, the one she'd met yesterday. The one she was beginning to like a little too much. "How do you know the sheriff? He arrest you for brawling?"

"Now that just plain hurt my feelings. What kind of guy do you take me for?"

"I was teasing."

And he knew it, judging by the smile tugging at his mouth. "I've been blowing through here for the last ten years or so. Craig and I met at some point along the way."

"You've come for the festival?"

"Mostly I've passed through on my way to a rodeo." Tanner squinted at an old green pickup that slowed in front of them. A young teenage girl hung halfway out the passenger window and yelled his name. A grin broke out across his face. "Is that you, Laura Kate? How did you get so pretty?"

"I have boobs now, too," she said, grinning back at him and pointing to her small chest.

Tanner scowled at her. "Get back in that truck."

Lexy almost choked on a cough. She was glad he hadn't encouraged the girl, who giggled, hollered that she'd see him later, then slid back to her seat.

"Jesus," Tanner muttered, a flush creeping up his neck and into his face.

It was kind of sweet. "Who was that?" Lexy asked.

"I know her brother. Billy's an amateur bareback rider." Shaking his head, Tanner glanced down the street after the pickup. "That kid's a handful. Glad I had only a brother to raise."

"You did?"

"No, not really. He was eight when our mom died and my grandparents took us in. Truthfully, they raised him. But I was his big brother, so…" He shrugged a shoulder, staring after the green truck. "Laura Kate's always been a real tomboy. Got it in her head early on she wanted to be a bull rider." He sighed. "Now she's thrilled about having boobs. I feel for Billy."

"I feel for anyone who has kids these days."

"Amen."

Lexy smiled, but she was disappointed he'd stopped talking about himself and his family. She wouldn't push, though. "I think my room is that way."

He released her elbow and for the briefest of moments she felt his hand at the small of her back. The gesture seemed oddly intimate, certainly more intimate than it should have. "You have the key?"

"I do," she said, wondering if he expected her to pass it to him. "I can take my bag now."

He just smiled and followed her to the orange door with number 112. Naturally, the key stuck, then the door, and he ended up using his shoulder to push it open. He winced and touched his arm.

"Hold on," he said when she started to go inside. He pulled the door closed again, triggering an automatic lock. Taking the key from her, he went through the entire process of unlocking and pushing the door open again. "We have to get you another room."

"We can't. This is the last one, bad plumbing and all."

Tanner frowned. "The plumbing doesn't work?"

"It does, but there's a problem with the hot water faucet." Lexy shrugged. "That's okay. It's only for one night."

He stared thoughtfully at her. "I don't think there's another motel in town but maybe we can find a bed and breakfast."

"I'm fine. Really." She stooped to get her bag but he stopped her. His palm felt slightly rough on her arm and her physical reaction to his touch made her swallow.

He closed the door again and stepped back. "Go ahead. You try."

"Oh, for goodness' sake." Easier to humor him, she decided, and used her shoulder as he had done. It was more difficult than she expected but the door opened. "Stronger than I look, huh?"

"No more tangling with you," he said, smiling when she rolled her eyes.

She walked into the room, startled by the bright green walls. The bed was a double and covered with the most god-awful blue-and-brown-plaid quilt. She couldn't imagine what kind of shape the mattress was in. The dresser and nightstand were small and cheap, constructed of particleboard, and the white plastic chair in the corner was more suited for an outdoor patio.

"This place sucks," Tanner said, his disdainful gaze sweeping the room. "You can sleep in the trailer and I'll stay here."

Lexy bit her lip. It would be mean to point out that his Betsy was only marginally better. "Do you have running water?"

"Course I do. I'm all hooked up." He ducked his head in the bathroom. "There's a tub and it looks clean."

Lifting her bag off the dresser where he'd left it, she studied the back of his broad shoulders and long legs. She doubted the plastic chair could even hold him. Not that she expected him to hang around.

"No offense to your buddy the sheriff, but his parents are crooks." She dropped the bag on the bed and unzipped it. "Before you showed up, they wanted a hundred and fifty dollars for the night. Can you believe that?"

Tanner turned around and saw that she was unpacking. "I'm serious about you taking the trailer."

"I appreciate the offer, but honestly, this is fine." She held up her toiletry bag, searching for signs of leakage from the heat. Everything looked all right. "At least the noise should be minimal this far back from the street."

She fished out her only pair of clean slacks and blouse so she could hang them, then realized Tanner had gotten quiet. He hadn't moved. He stood in the bathroom doorway, his gaze fixed on the bed. Or more precisely, on the red silk thong and matching bra she'd unthinkingly laid out.

"Dinner." Tanner's eyes slowly met hers. "What time should I come by?"

The room suddenly seemed stuffy. Lexy spotted the thermostat control and went to adjust the air conditioner. "You go without me," she said, glad to have something other than him to focus on. "I'm really not hungry."

"Six-thirty it is, then."

"Fine," she said, wanting him gone before she did something stupid.

"Okay." He lifted the hat off his head and resettled it, tugging the rim low as he walked to the door. "By the way, I think you just turned on the heat."

She stared at the thermostat. "No," she said, trying not to give in to a smile. "It's just you."

9

TANNER OPENED THE door for Lexy, then followed her inside the restaurant. She'd left her hair down, the honey-gold streaks catching rays from the late-afternoon sun. He was glad she hadn't changed out of the snug-fitting jeans, and without being a total prick, he studied her butt trying to figure out if she was wearing the red thong.

The place was crowded and noisy, most of the raucous laughter coming from the bar. He'd warned her that they might have to wait for a table. She hadn't seemed bothered. The woman continued to surprise him. If he hadn't seen her driver's license for himself, he never would've believed she was a Worthington. People like that didn't stay in shabby motels. And certainly not without complaining. Lexy hadn't even blinked at the ugly room.

Two occupied wooden benches sat on either side of the tiled entryway. Probably folks waiting for tables. Three women were checking out the menu. He already knew what he wanted.

They stepped up to the sign telling them a hostess would seat them, and Tanner got a peek at the wait list on the podium. Looked as if it was gonna be a while.

"Wow, that smells good." She leaned close so he could

hear, and the seductive scent of her perfume hit him low in the belly.

"Rib eye," he said, his voice rough enough he had to clear his throat.

"I don't care what it is, I'm having it." She was about to pluck a laminated menu from the stack when the blonde hostess greeted them.

Tanner had fully expected to wait an hour, but he didn't argue when the woman led them to a small table in the far back. Seconds later a perky brunette told them her name was Sandy and took their drink order.

"Okay, this is weird. I thought for sure we'd have to wait," Lexy said.

"Me, too."

"I think the blonde likes you."

"Yeah?" He was sorry that he couldn't see Lexy's eyes more clearly in the dim corner. In the daylight they looked so blue.

"Oh, brother, are you that used to women falling all over you?"

"What are you talking about?"

"I mention the blonde and you're so blasé." She tilted her head slightly to the side and studied him. "You should really consider doing the calendar. I think you'll rake in the votes."

And here he thought they could have a nice evening. "Keep it down," he muttered, then smiled at Sandy when she brought his beer and Lexy's iced tea.

"These are on Buddy," she said, throwing a glance toward the bar. "Ready to order? Or should I come back?"

He knew only one Buddy, a bull rider who'd been sidelined several years ago by a skull fracture. "Cooper?"

"That's him."

"What's he doing?" Tanner asked, unable to spot him. "Drinking?"

"Working." Sandy grinned. "And probably some drinking. He bought the place last year. The bartender just got slammed with orders so Buddy's helping out."

"Tell him I'll come see him in a bit."

"Will do."

Tanner let Lexy order first, amazed that she hadn't customized her entrée. The steak came with grilled onions and the potato with butter and sour cream. She wanted everything. All he had to do was tell Sandy he'd have the same.

"I guess that's why we didn't have to wait," Lexy said, her eyes on the platters of food being served at the next table. "Your friend must've seen you walk in. I swear, you know everyone." She brought her gaze back to his. "What?"

He picked up his beer and took a long sip. She'd caught him staring. He could tell her he thought she had the prettiest blue eyes he'd ever seen. It was the truth, but it might ruin dinner if she thought he was hitting on her. "I'm wondering where you're gonna put all that food you ordered."

"Oh, don't worry about that. I can eat."

"Wait till you see the portions."

She glanced at the next table and laughed. "I was just hoping that my potato will be that big."

He smiled. "I can't imagine what your appetite is like when you're actually hungry."

Her brief glare ended on a sigh. "Okay, I deserved that one. I hate being in this situation. I swear I'm usually more professional. And of course you know I'll pay you back for both our dinners. Remind me to get a receipt."

"Don't worry about it. I never let a woman pay."

Her slack-jawed reaction came right on cue. Now, the way she swiped her tongue seductively across her lip...that he hadn't expected. "This isn't a date."

"You ever go out with a cowboy?"

Lexy's brows went up. "Where on earth did that come from?"

"Or do you go for guys in designer suits with expensive haircuts and fancy cars?"

"I don't have a type…not really." She seemed to be giving the matter serious thought. "If my father disapproved of a man, that was good enough for me. But that was when I was younger," she said, grabbing her tea and taking a sip, looking like a woman who wished she hadn't let that little piece of info slip out.

"You get along with him now?"

"Mostly. What about you?"

He plowed a hand through his hair. Weird not wearing his Stetson, but he never did in restaurants. "I see the old man from time to time, though I can't say I have much use for him. My mom died twenty years ago."

"I'm sorry. She must've been young."

"Yep." All this time and he still had trouble talking about her, forget trying to control the surge of anger toward his father. To Tanner's way of thinking, the man had been as responsible as if he'd pulled the trigger himself. "Too young to die, that's for sure."

She hesitated, and he said a silent prayer that she would drop the subject. "And you have just the one brother?"

"Yep. We're different as night and day, but we get along well. Doug's also my attorney," Tanner said, watching her face as the words sunk in. He tried not to laugh. "I told him you suggested he be replaced."

Her lips parted. "Dear God, please tell me you're kidding."

Tanner liked that she cared about his brother's feelings. "Isn't that what you said?"

"Yes, but I didn't know he was your brother."

"Business is business," he said, shrugging and watching her worry her lower lip.

"Are you going to fire him?"

"Doug thought he was looking out for me. Can't fault

him for that." He saw that she was dying to comment, probably thought he was being a fool. But he wasn't about to set
her straight. Point out that his brother had foreseen Tanner's rodeo career hitting the skids.

"I'm assuming he told you the contract is binding."

"Our conversation is privileged."

Lexy's smile stretched wide. "I'll take that as a yes."

Sandy showed up with a basket of rolls that she set on
the table. The smell alone was enough to make his stomach growl. He waited for Lexy to dig in but all she did was
stare at the red-and-white-checkered napkin draped over
the basket.

"Go for it," she said finally. "I'm saving room."

"Are you insane?" He shook his head, grabbed the but-
tery-looking roll and slathered more butter on it. "I see
Buddy hasn't changed anything. These are homemade and
still warm."

"Screw it." She got her own roll, tore off a big piece and
stuffed it in her mouth.

"Atta girl." He had to laugh.

"Shut up. I never get to eat this kind of food. My roommate would have a stroke if I brought anything non-organic
into the apartment."

"Roommate?"

She nodded, held up a finger and continued to chew.
After she swallowed, she said, "I know, it's pretty sad someone my age needing a roommate. It's not so bad. Linda's a
pilot so she's gone a lot."

Lexy *needed* a roommate? That didn't make sense. She
had to be pulling in some serious money working for the
family business.

He put down his roll and took another sip of beer.

"Yes, I have a trust fund," she said quietly, dabbing at
her mouth with the cloth napkin. "That's what you were
wondering, right?"

"Sort of…I reckon."

"I can't touch it until I'm thirty." She sighed. "Well, no, I can, but not without the consent of both my parents."

"I'm guessing you don't want to ask."

She blew out a puff of air. "I'd rather climb up on this table and dance naked."

He almost spit out his beer. "Thanks for that visual."

"You're welcome."

"You're a cruel woman, Alexis."

"Yes, but it's a hard, cold world." Her smile was really something. It lit her face with a warm glow he could feel across the table. "I like you, Tanner," she said softly. "I didn't expect that."

Before he could tell her the feeling was mutual, Sandy appeared with their salads. Probably just as well. He really did like Lexy, enough that he was starting to feel uneasy.

To her credit, she hadn't waited for him to return the declaration. She'd gone to work drizzling blue-cheese dressing lightly over the lettuce and tomatoes. It was quite a production. Took him two seconds to drench his salad.

They ate in silence until the steaks arrived. He was happy to swap plates with Sandy, but Lexy hung on to her salad, finishing the greens in between enthusiastic bites of steak and potato. It bothered him that he'd let her get that hungry. Course she was an adult, and besides, he'd had no way of knowing she was low on money. But he was no stranger to stubborn pride. If not for the motel incident, she'd probably be eating junk out of the vending machine.

"You're right," she said, putting her fork down. "Best steak ever."

"I seem to recall they serve a mean peach cobbler."

"One more bite and I'm going to explode."

"You haven't finished."

She eyed the half-eaten meal. "I'm taking the rest with

me. Crappy as that motel is, there's a microwave in the room."

"I've got one in the trailer, too. We'll order the cobbler to go."

A smile lifted the corners of her mouth. "Put it on my tab."

"How about I take it out in trade?"

She blinked, let out a soft laugh. "I beg your pardon."

"Shoulda known you'd show up eventually." Buddy's voice seemed to come out of nowhere.

Tanner hadn't seen him approach but he felt the man's beefy hand clap him on the back. Before he could turn around, Buddy pulled out a chair and sat down. He held a pair of beer bottles by the necks and set one next to Tanner's empty.

With a half smile, Tanner moved the rolls and butter to give him room. "Sure, Buddy, why don't you join us?"

"Christ, Tanner, how long has it been? Two years?" Buddy's eyes were bloodshot and he had a paunch on him. He was younger than Tanner but he looked as if he'd been barreling down a few miles of bad road.

"At least. I just heard you bought the place."

"Yeah, well, I had to find something to do. It ain't rodeoing, but it keeps me in beer and out of jail."

Tanner looked at Lexy, about to introduce her when Buddy said, "And what's your name, darlin'?"

Oh, she loved that, Tanner thought, watching her dab the napkin at the corner of her mouth. He could read her well enough to know she was stalling, figuring out how to respond. She wouldn't want to embarrass him, but she sure as hell didn't like being called *darlin'*.

"Lexy," she said finally.

"Pretty name for a pretty lady," Buddy said, and glanced at her iced tea. "How about something stronger? Sandy will go get anything you want."

Lexy's smile was very polite, very controlled. "And you are?"

"Buddy Cooper, bull rider extraordinaire, at your service." He picked up her hand and kissed the back.

Her eyes widened a fraction but she kept the smile in place, withdrew her hand and lowered it to her lap.

"Extraordi— What?" Tanner asked, then winked at Lexy.

"Don't mind him," Buddy said, leaning forward, his forearms pressed to the table. "He's what us cultured folks call uncouth."

Tanner laughed. "Lucinda must be teaching you all those fancy words."

"Ah, hell, she left me two years ago." Buddy straightened and sighed. "Don't marry a buckle bunny, Tanner. No matter how pretty or how sweet-smelling she is, don't you do it. The minute the fat paychecks dry up and she knows there won't be any more shiny gold buckles, she'll be gone so fast it'll give you whiplash." He rubbed his eyes. "Shit, Lucinda couldn't even wait till I recovered from that last surgery."

"I'm sorry," Tanner said, all too familiar with the scenario.

"Hey, no worries… This place keeps me busy, so it's all good." Buddy smiled at Lexy. "We were about to get you a real drink, darlin'. What'll it be?"

"I'm fine, but thank you." She didn't seem put off this time. When she turned to him, Tanner caught a glint of sympathy in her eyes. "If you two would like to catch up, I don't mind going back to my room. I have several calls to make."

"No," Tanner said, irritated that he sounded curt. But he wanted to spend time with her. "Let's go walk off some of this dinner. I'll come back and visit Buddy later when he's not so busy."

"You're not in the game?" Buddy said, looking over his

shoulder when someone called for him. "I figured that's why you were here."

Lexy glared at him, but he honestly didn't know what Buddy meant. "What game?"

"Texas Hold 'em. Ten grand buy-in."

"Hell, I don't play for that kind of money. You know that."

Buddy pushed back from the table, grinning at Lexy. "If you don't already know, this guy's a cheapskate."

Tanner snorted and reached in his pocket. "Yeah, because I don't give my money away at poker."

"You still got that old tin-can trailer?"

Tanner signaled Sandy for the bill. "You watch how you talk about Betsy. She's been more faithful than—" He caught himself, but it was too late. Buddy could easily fill in the blanks. It was obvious Tanner had been joking, but man, he felt like shit.

Buddy waved a hand and got to his feet. "You're right about that. Like I said, it's all good. Now put your money away. Better learn to take a free dinner when it's offered. I heard you've been achin' in a lotta new places lately."

Knowing Buddy meant no harm didn't take the sting out of the reminder. "Dinner is on Lexy. Right, darlin'?" Tanner emphasized the endearment and grinned at the daggers shooting from her eyes.

Then her lips curved in a smile that managed to come across like a one-finger salute.

"Well now, that sounds mighty interesting." Buddy pushed the chair in, his flushed face full of curiosity. "Somebody lose a wager?"

"I'll come by later," Tanner said quickly. Too late he realized he shouldn't have invited questions about Lexy. He didn't need the guys razzing him about the calendar. "Is the game gonna be here?"

"In the back room right after the restaurant closes.

Lance, Cortez and Travis are coming for sure. A few more maybes. I'm not expecting J.D. since he's still kicking ass down in Milford. He won't wanna mess with his mojo. Can't say as I blame him, though I wouldn't mind taking some of that cash off him." Buddy turned when he got another shout from the bar. "I gotta go."

Tanner said nothing while they waited for the check and Lexy's to-go box. He was still thinking about J.D. sitting in the catbird seat down in Colorado. He really had to be packing some luck. The man didn't have money for high-stakes poker. Those games were set up for the big boys with fat wallets. Tanner hoped he was still flush because J.D. would never leave a game while on a winning streak. That left the path clear for Tanner to come back later to see the guys. He'd managed to avoid J.D. for seven months now, and he aimed to keep it that way.

"He's quite a character," Lexy said, breaking into his thoughts.

"Who?"

"Buddy."

"Yeah, he's got a wicked sense of humor. When he was younger he used to play locker room practical jokes. Made a lot of enemies. Everyone's got their rituals before riding. They don't want anyone messing with them."

"What's yours?"

He saw Sandy headed toward them, and was never so glad to get a bill in his life. Yeah, he knew the question was just idle curiosity. But he never discussed his silly superstitious routine with anyone. Although it sure hadn't been doing him any good lately.

Sandy brought him the check, and he glanced at the total, then gave it back to her with a hundred-dollar bill.

"May I have a receipt, please?" Lexy asked.

"No, she doesn't need one."

"Yes, I do."

Tanner sighed. "Don't we have enough to argue about… can we let this one go?"

She glared at him for a second, then murmured, "You forgot to order the peach cobbler."

Sandy grinned. "I'm on it. One or two pieces?"

"Two," they said at the same time.

As soon as she left, Lexy asked, "Your ritual?"

He shook his head. "Not gonna happen."

"You won't tell me?"

"Nope."

"Is it something embarrassing?"

After draining his beer, he threw his napkin on the table. "It's private."

She looked far too interested and not the least put off by his brusque tone. "Does anyone know what it is?"

He hesitated. No point lying. "Yes. One person."

"Who?"

"None of your business."

"Okay, that means female," she said, looking pleased with herself as if she'd solved a major mystery. "A girl-friend?"

"No, but she had to sleep with me to get the information."

As he suspected, that shut her up.

But it didn't stop her from studying him with narrowed eyes. Part of him wanted to know what was going on in that conniving brain of hers, but the logical part convinced him to leave it alone.

Sandy brought their cobbler and the change, which he told her to keep, earning him an arched brow from Lexy. Yeah, so what if he'd overtipped? It was his money. She wasn't paying him back for dinner.

They both stood, and though he hoped Lexy would take the lead, she waited for him. "I have another question," she said as they walked shoulder to shoulder to the door.

"You'll say it's none of my business but I really would like to know."

"Go ahead."

"Does it bother you when someone implies your career is almost over?"

Jesus. Tanner hesitated. "Yeah, it bothers me."

"I'm sorry."

"That's life," he said, shrugging, then reached around her to open the door.

She stopped right in the doorway and looked up at him with uncertainty in those heart-stopping blue eyes. "You were right yesterday," she said with a small sigh. "I did piss off Daddy."

10

LEXY WASN'T QUITE sure why she'd made the admission. Except she'd been touched by Tanner's candor and she wanted to give him something in return.

They'd stepped outside but were still blocking the entrance. He took her arm and drew her toward the parking lot. She switched the doggie bag to her other hand, and they wove around parked cars and monster trucks, not stopping until they got to the sidewalk.

"Do you want to talk about it?" he asked, relieving her of the bag.

She stared at him for a long moment, then shook her head. "It's very boring and even more clichéd." She liked being able to look at him this closely. He had a good face, well-shaped lips, strong jaw. Even cleanly shaven he had a ruggedly handsome thing going on. She wondered if she would've given him a second look had they passed each other on an Oklahoma City street.

Her first instinct was a resounding yes. Though in truth, probably not. Lots of guys wore boots and cowboy hats downtown. They never caught her eye. But now that she knew Tanner a little, it was impossible to tell.

"You still interested in taking a walk?" He touched her

face, jerking her back to the conversation. All he did was tuck an unruly curl behind her ear.

"Where?"

"A few blocks south is the festival grounds. They'll have game booths, food concessions, a band playing. Probably even a dance floor."

"Is that supposed to tempt me?"

He grinned. "I hope not."

"You're safe, cowboy." She laughed and patted his chest. The casual, unthinking touch started a jitter in her tummy. He was solid muscle and his heart pounded nearly as fast as hers.

"Or we could go back to your room," he said, his hazel eyes turning a chocolate brown.

"And do what, exactly?"

"Hard to explain." He leaned in and brushed his lips below her ear. "I'd have to show you," he whispered, his husky voice caressing her skin.

This so wasn't fair. Oh, God, this should've been a simple no-brainer errand. Find a cowboy for the calendar…a man who shouldn't appeal to her in the least…deliver him to the photo shoot. Fly back to Oklahoma City solo. The end. Easy as…

She heard a soft whimper and blinked. Had the sound come from her? Amazed, she straightened and moved back a step. She saw that he still held on to the bag and his other hand remained at his side. Only his lips had touched her. How was that possible? Her entire body felt flushed, tingly.

Her hand was still pressed to his chest, and she calmly removed it, ignoring the slight tremor in her fingers. In a matter of seconds, daylight seemed to slip into dusk, shadowing his face and cloaking them in an intimate cocoon.

"It doesn't have to be anything heavy," he said, brushing the hair away from her eyes. "Maybe a little kissing, talking…" He smiled. "More kissing."

"You know it won't stop there."

"We're adults. We can stop any time we want."

The want was the thing that worried her. He didn't understand, and she couldn't expect him to know how important it was that she not screw up. Sex she could get anywhere. But sex with him…as incredible as the experience would undoubtedly be…could end badly. Any hint that she'd behaved unprofessionally and it was over for her. No more second chances. Her father didn't give them readily, and this was it.

On the other hand, she'd already seen Tanner naked. And she wouldn't mind seeing more of that.

Dammit.

"Kissing. Only kissing," she said, jittery at how intensely he was focused on her mouth. "Any touching has to be through clothes. Agreed?"

He lifted his gaze and laughed. "Do I have to sign somewhere?"

"This isn't a joke." She shuddered for no reason. The air was cool but not cold. At his troubled look, she murmured, "I know you don't understand."

"How about we walk and talk?" He slipped an arm around her shoulders, and she really should've objected instead of leaning her head against him.

They walked along the busy highway, against traffic that flowed steadily in the opposite direction toward the festival grounds. A few people honked their horns, whether randomly or because they recognized Tanner, it was hard to say. He'd been stopped for autographs a lot.

At first his popularity had confused her because she didn't understand the rodeo world. But it pleased her, as well, since it meant he was a viable candidate that would make her look good. And then she'd started resenting the intrusions, which should've told her that she might be in trouble. A young boy had stopped him on their way to the restaurant. He never turned down signing autographs for kids, no matter how inconvenient.

The boy was chatty and excited to meet his hero, and what had she done? Waited impatiently, glancing at her watch, and in general, acting much like the spoiled brats she'd detested in boarding school. Fortunately, Tanner hadn't noticed. If he had, it would've shamed her.

"You're quiet," he said. "Having second thoughts?"

"So are you. Quiet, I mean."

He tightened his hold around her shoulders, forcing her to lean on him. "Oh, I'm having plenty of thoughts. I doubt you want to hear them."

Wanna bet? was her knee-jerk response. But that was the other Lexy, the untamed one who'd gotten her into this predicament with her father. "Probably not."

"That isn't what you wanted to say."

"You're a mind reader now?"

"Body language, sweetheart. Remember? It's much more reliable than words."

She gave him a light shove. "Sweetheart. Darlin'. What's with you cowboys? Is using a woman's name too much of a commitment?"

"Well, seems like I hit a couple of nerves." Tanner lowered his arm. "Didn't mean to ruffle your feathers."

"Oh, please, you didn't even come close." She hadn't meant for him to release her.

"All right, then you won't mind my suggesting you work on your breathing. That was the real giveaway."

She stopped and looked at him. "Remind me why I like you."

Tanner grinned. "That's progress. Yesterday you wanted to pull a shotgun on me."

Lexy laughed and sighed at the same time. "Of course I like you or I wouldn't have kissed you."

"Speaking of which, can you walk a little faster?"

Words escaped her. In some ways, he made things easy. Too easy. She slid an arm around his waist, and he put his arm back around her shoulders. He set a brisk pace, and she did her best to keep up.

"We'd better be careful," she said when they reached the motel and were close to her room. "If Vivian knows you're with me, she'll charge double."

She'd been joking, of course, and turned to see why he hadn't responded. He was looking at her, just looking. No smile, no anything.

"Tanner?"

He set the bag on the ground and took her face in his hands. She backed up against the cool brick, using the wall for support. Foolish, really, when she had his broad shoulders to hold on to.

She tentatively moved her hands. "You know my room is only seconds away, right?"

"I know," he murmured, his lips skimming hers, then warming the sensitive skin below her jaw. He returned to her mouth, kissing her leisurely at first, taking his time until he found an angle to his liking. And then he coaxed her lips apart with a skillfulness that had her quivering.

He swept his tongue inside her mouth, swirling and teasing and leaving his brand in every nook. She normally wasn't a passive partner but she just stood there, spellbound, her heart pounding, while she soaked in the taste and masculine smell of him.

When he moved his lips to her neck, a split second of reason left her with an awful thought. He'd changed his mind. He wasn't coming inside. This was a good-night kiss.

"Tanner." She hated how weak her voice sounded, but it was the best she could do. "Why?"

He lifted his head and looked at her, his calloused thumb stroking her jaw over and over. "I couldn't wait."

She squinted as if that would help her understand. "What?"

"I'm sorry." He lowered his hand and turned his gaze toward the street. "I didn't mean to get—" Sheepishly, he rubbed the back of his neck. "That wasn't cool. I should've waited until we got inside."

Laughter bubbled up and spilled out. "Are you kidding? That was totally cool."

He studied her for a moment, then put out his hand. "Key."

By the time she passed it to him, he'd scooped up the bag and planted a quick kiss on her mouth. He inserted the key then muttered a curse when it didn't work.

"The next room is mine," she said, still laughing, then pushed him when he couldn't understand her garbled words.

His muscled arms were hard as stone and she had to use all her strength to get him to move. He finally realized his mistake and only shook his head. Apparently, he didn't find the situation as funny as she did.

"Hurry up before my neighbors call security."

"That would be Craig. No problem." He turned the key in the lock.

She pushed open the door and rushed inside. "Yeah, fine, he won't arrest *you*."

Tanner followed and kicked the door closed behind him. "You'd look cute in jailhouse stripes," he said, running his gaze down the front of her blouse. "Although if I had my druthers—"

"Wait. Stop. Only kissing, remember?"

"And you're reminding me now because…?"

"You were about to say naked. That you'd rather see me naked. Weren't you?"

He set the bag on top of the microwave and gave her a slow, sexy smile that made her clench everything from her teeth to her toes. "So let's review the rules—only kissing.

Any touching has to be done through clothes. And now no talking."

Lexy laughed. "It sounds crazy when you put it like that." She switched on the lamp, then tugged the curtains together so that they overlapped. "I wish we had another chair."

Tanner caught her hand. He drew her closer, watching her nervously moisten her lips. "We have a bed."

"You know the rules."

"Yes, I do." He circled his arms around her, making her feel small and helpless and shockingly excited.

She tipped her head back to look into his eyes. They were so dark, so damn hungry, it sent a jolt down her spine. His breath, though, was warm and steady, too steady, while she could scarcely breathe. His mouth was damp and even more tempting now that she knew what it could do. She lowered her lashes. If she kept looking at him, she'd eventually toss the rules out the window.

He nudged her chin farther up until she was gazing at him again. He said nothing, only touched her face with the back of his hand, lightly grazing her cheek with his knuckles. She stayed perfectly still, one hand at her side, the other clutching a fistful of his shirt while he brushed his thumb across her mouth.

"So soft," he murmured, his voice barely audible, his breath coming quicker. He lowered his head and his lips took over for his thumb.

Impatient, she released his shirt and wound her arms around his neck. Her breasts pushed against his chest. She felt his hands move down her back, cup her butt and pull her closer. His arousal pressed hard, urgent and hot, the heat penetrating the denim of their jeans.

The clothes were supposed to stop them from doing anything foolish. It wasn't working. Not when his tongue swirled and mated with hers, tasting and teasing. And his hands… God, even the way he gently squeezed her ass made her want to rip his shirt off.

Tightening her hold around his neck, she slipped a hand between their bodies and touched his bulging fly. Tanner pulled her arms away and stopped kissing her. Lexy stumbled back a step. She looked at his face, frustrated that she couldn't read him.

"Okay, new rules," she said, then gasped when he scooped her up and carried her to the bed.

He set her down on the mattress and started unbuttoning his shirt. "Yeah," he said, jerking the hem from his jeans. "I've never been much for toeing the line."

"You agreed," she protested, her voice lacking conviction. Because…well…she was watching him shrug out of his shirt and staring at his bare chest and no one could expect her to think straight. No one.

Except her father.

The thought knocked the wind out of her.

"Wait." She bolted upright. "Just wait."

"You're right. I agreed." He tossed his shirt at the chair, then sat on the edge of the bed and pulled off a boot. "I just didn't know how far you were willing to bend those silly rules of yours." He removed the second boot and looked her in the eye. "I promise I won't do anything you don't want me to do. But I'm warning you, Lexy, I'm not a damn saint."

She rarely blushed but she did now. The way she'd rubbed him…okay, that was on her.

"You wanna discuss new rules?" he said, and she noticed he'd left on his socks. "Let's go."

The sensual fog had mostly lifted. Her head was clear enough for her to admit this was a horrible idea. She should tell him she'd made a mistake, beg for his forgiveness and discretion. Her gaze went to his chest, the swell of his pectoral muscles, the pair of flat, brown nipples.

"All right, topless is okay." She yanked her blouse from her waistband and pulled it off.

Staring at her red bra, he took her blouse, threw it, missing the chair by a mile. "Please tell me the bra comes off, too."

Lexy sighed. She'd only worn the shirt to dinner and it was her last clean one. But when she looked at Tanner's heated expression, she didn't give a damn.

"Too slow." He stretched across the bed and reached behind her. "The bra goes," he said, and with a single flick of the clasp, the cups loosened but stayed in place.

"I see you've done this before," she said, laughing, impressed with his dexterity and speed.

"Not going there." He clearly wasn't happy with the comment, but then he leaned back, staring at her breasts with laser focus, as if he could will the bra to fall off.

She hadn't meant anything, but maybe he was touchy about the whole buckle-bunny phenomenon. Afraid he'd grow impatient and rip the delicate silk, Lexy slipped the straps off her shoulders and set the bra aside.

The slight flare of his nostrils as he reached for her sent her pulse soaring. He palmed one breast, then the other. He circled her nipple with his thumb, and she bit her lip to keep from moaning.

"Anything else you want to take off?" he asked, his voice low and raspy. Without waiting for an answer, he kissed her breast while he toyed with her other nipple, his fingers flicking the pearled tip.

When he finally drew her into his mouth, she shuddered, and arched against his tongue. In an instant, he'd shoved the pillows against the headboard, flipped onto his back and took her with him. His arms came around her so that her breasts were crushed against his bare chest.

He trailed his lips up the side of her neck, lightly bit her earlobe, then found her mouth. The kiss started out slow, very sensual, soft nibbles, a swipe of the tongue, their mouths exploring and resettling. It had been a very long time since Lexy had been kissed this way, as if the kissing itself was the prize and not leading to something else. He sucked her bottom lip into his mouth so gently it made her ache. His hand skimmed the curve of her hip, then retraced the path to cup her breast.

Not for a second did he stop kissing her. Sometimes closed-mouthed, more often open, but always determined. Almost as if he couldn't get enough of her. He moved his hands a lot, though, touching everything that was exposed, lingering in certain sensitive places as if he knew that particular spot would drive her crazy. He slid a fingertip under her waistband, and she sucked in a breath.

He stopped kissing her and rolled over again until she was on her back. His eyes were nearly black when he looked down at her. "Stay right here," he said and rose from the bed.

Tanner unbuckled his belt.

She squeezed her thighs together. "What are you doing?"

"Just getting rid of the buckle," he said, pulling the belt free of his jeans. "That's all. I don't want it to hurt you."

Lexy nodded, wondering if he noticed her disappointment. Or how she was staring at the impressive bulge behind his fly. She lifted her gaze to his face. He was too busy checking her out.

He dropped the belt on the floor, then slid his body up hers until their mouths met. The friction of his chest rubbing her nipples pushed her too close to the edge. Her pitiful whimper had him lifting his head.

Looking into her eyes, he brushed a strand of hair from her face and smiled. "You okay?"

His borderline arrogance should've annoyed her. He damn well knew she was all right, and he was torturing her. Trying to get her to rescind the rules. She just wished she had a witty retort at the ready.

Concern furrowing his brows, he eased back. "Am I too heavy? I thought I was supporting most of my weight."

"No." So she'd misread him. "No. I—" Oh, God, she was such a hypocrite. "I was hoping you wouldn't stop with your belt."

"You're not being fair." He leaned back. "I told you we can keep this low key, but don't ask me to lie here naked with you and not expect me to want to be inside you."

"Oh." She swallowed, felt around for the covers to pull up, then remembered they were lying on top of the quilt. "I'm being totally unprofessional. I apologize. I got carried away."

He stilled her frantic hands, closing his much larger one over both of them. "Is that why you're holding back? You think it's unprofessional?"

"Of course it is."

"My contract expires in a matter of days. This whole thing is a farce. The only reason I'm going to Houston is so I won't be sued. I guarantee you I will never agree to being in the calendar no matter how much money your company throws at me."

"I know," she admitted, feeling guilty that she'd threatened him with the phony lawsuit. Setting him straight now, though, could make him angry. "I do."

"Realistically, we don't have a professional relationship." He brought her hand to his lips and kissed the back of her knuckles. "Which leaves two consenting adults who both seem pretty damn-attracted to each other."

"My company wouldn't see it that way."

"Who would know? You plan on telling someone?"

"Oh, God, no," she said, and a wry smile curved his mouth.

She understood what he was saying...what he didn't get

was how she absolutely could not displease her father. It didn't matter. The decision was hers to make. She didn't know Tanner well enough to trust he wouldn't use this thing between them to hurt her, but she trusted her instinct. He was one of the good guys. She hadn't had too many of them in her life. Did she really want to ignore the possibility that tonight could be something wonderful?

"If you want me to leave, no problem." He dropped a gentle kiss on her lips. "I'd like to stay, but if it makes you uncomfortable, I'll go, and tomorrow we'll pick up where we left off at dinner." He smiled. "I'll even buy you break-fast."

His low, soothing voice and willingness to be gracious was enough to convince her she needed tonight with this man. He kept his gaze above her shoulders, his hand over hers. No matter what she said he wouldn't pressure her. He'd be a complete gentleman.

"Yes," she whispered. "I want you to stay."

"Thank God," he said, his chest heaving slightly.

A happy flush warmed her. Had he been holding his breath waiting for her response? Had she done that to him? Tanner always seemed so calm.

"I do have a small problem," he said grimly, and she didn't like the sound of that. "I don't have a condom. Not on me. I have a box in the trailer."

"I think I might have one." She scooted off the bed. "It's been a while but it should be okay." She stopped searching her purse and looked at him. "You realized you didn't have a condom when we got to the door, didn't you? That's why you hesitated."

A smile tugged at his mouth. "Yeah, but then I remembered the only-kissing rule, so it didn't matter."

Lexy sighed. Tanner was the real deal. A true gentleman, the kind of guy with whom she'd better be very careful. She threw the packet to him, then unzipped her jeans.

11

BEFORE LEXY FINISHED wiggling out of her jeans, Tanner had stripped his off along with his boxers. He was pulling the quilt down to the foot of the bed by the time she stood only in her red thong. The heated way he tracked her with his eyes made her feel like the sexiest woman on earth.

"Dammit, I should've gone to get the box while I was still dressed."

She laughed. "You really think we'll need more than one condom?"

"You don't?" He seemed genuinely shocked, and put a fist to his heart. "You wound me."

"Then I guess I have a lot of ego-stroking to do," she said, glancing at his erection.

He broke out in a boyish grin. "Oh, yeah."

He came around the bed and laid her down on the mattress. The sheets were terrible, made of a cheap, rough cotton, but that ceased to matter when he pulled off her panties. He had no problem taking his time, looking his fill. Then he kissed her below her belly button. The unexpected move made her squeeze her legs together.

Bringing his head up, he searched her face. "Anything you don't like, you tell me."

"I will." She wasn't shy about that sort of thing. "You

surprised me, that's all," she said, parting her thighs a little. "Don't hold back. I trust you."

His slow smile was different than any other he'd given her. He kissed the same spot near her belly button, then pressed a second kiss between her ribs, and left a damp trail up to her breasts. She combed her fingers through his hair, giving it a good yank when he sucked a nipple into his mouth.

With amusement in his eyes, he glanced up. "Does that mean stop or do it some more?"

She laughed. "Get up here where I can reach you."

He did what she asked while slipping a hand between her thighs. Of course she was damp. No, not just damp, but wet and slick, and his body shuddered against hers as he explored her with his fingers.

"God, Alexis," he murmured, rubbing his lips across her breasts and stroking her until she had to squeeze her thighs together again.

Her name had never been said like that before. She could hardly breathe from wanting him. And since she'd managed to trap his hand where she was most sensitive, she found no respite from his skillful touch.

His chin came up and he covered her mouth with his, thrusting his tongue between her lips, his kiss so savage that her heart pounded and the blood raced through her veins. She clutched more of his hair, and was shocked to realize her other hand was clawing at his shoulder.

She tried to relax, tried to breathe in deeply. But he inserted one long finger inside her and she almost came off the mattress. She turned away from his kiss. Without missing a beat he moved his mouth to her neck, but she had her own agenda. The trouble was, he'd already figured out she was super sensitive where her shoulder and neck met, and he wouldn't ease up.

Slipping her hand down his chest, she bypassed his belly

and gripped his cock. Hard and hot, it pulsed against her palm. "I can feel your heartbeat."

"Hmm," Tanner said, his head rolling back as she ran her hand down his shaft and slowly back up again.

"It's beating awfully fast."

He righted himself until his heavy-lidded gaze met hers. "I'm a professional athlete, sweetheart. I'm just getting started."

Her pulse quickened at the notion and the feel of him in her grip. Or maybe it was his insistent thumb. She tried to hold back a moan but gave in after he circled the sensitive nub with just enough pressure to drive her mad.

"A little tight," he murmured, his voice sounding funny.

She let go of him completely. "Did I hurt you?"

He shook his head and smiled. "I knew I shouldn't tangle with a woman like you."

"I am a force to be reckoned with." She couldn't help but jerk as his thumb resumed his teasing.

He laughed as he bent to kiss her again. "I think I can handle things from my end." He moved until he loomed over her, his thigh sneaking between her legs, urging them to spread farther.

She obeyed willingly. The only sparring she was interested in was verbal, but if he kept kissing her like that, she'd have no breath left.

"I know how you can make it up to me," he said, his mouth so close to hers they almost brushed.

"Whatever I can do."

"That condom is about an inch from your left knee. If you'd be so kind as to hand it to me."

"So soon?"

"Not quite," he said, sliding down her body with amazing dexterity, considering he still had one finger inside her. He sucked her right nipple as he moved, then nibbled on her hip bone and licked the crease where her thigh began.

Lexy found the condom, and since he had no free hands, she put it on her belly, within easy reach. Then she didn't think about it again because she felt his hot breath sneak inside her as he spread her lower lips.

She'd thought his thumb was talented. His mouth made her yank the bottom sheet from beneath the mattress. She knew she was being loud and that the walls had to be paper thin, but she couldn't make herself care. He played her like a maestro, taking her to the edge, then easing back until she was ready to beg.

Maybe he heard the desperation in her voice, or perhaps it was the way she was trembling so hard she thought she might fly apart. Whatever it was, he stayed focused. God, did he focus.

She came with a spasm that made the bed bang against the wall.

Before she could see or breathe again, she heard the tear of the condom package and his deep, rumbling moan as he lifted her leg until it rested on his shoulder. Then he was inside her. Thick and hot and filling her as she quaked and moaned, tumbling toward another orgasm.

Unexpectedly he withdrew, his movement slow, measured. She heard their panting breaths mingle as she waited for the hard thrust that would fill her again, banish the emptiness that had been mounting deep inside her. Turning his head, he kissed the inner part of her ankle where it lay on his shoulder. Then he smiled at her and started moving again, in and out with restrained little thrusts that tested her patience.

"Please, Tanner," she whispered, reaching for his hips, trying to force him to push in deeper.

"Don't you want it to last?" he asked hoarsely.

"No."

The single, harshly panted word was all it took. He thrust into her as if his control had suddenly snapped, then pushed again with enough force to steal her breath, leaving her defenseless against the rush of sensations overtaking her.

The world shimmered and soared behind her closed lids, and when she heard him groan, felt his body shudder, she had just enough strength for her inner muscles to squeeze his cock.

At least this time, there were no complaints.

TANNER KNEW THE sun hadn't come up yet, though he suspected it was morning. The muted glow from a streetlight spilled past the curtains, making it hard to gauge the time. Behind him the digital alarm clock sat on the nightstand. But if he moved, he'd wake Lexy, and he wasn't willing to do that. Neither of them had slept much.

With her cheek pressed against his chest, he shifted just a little so his arm wouldn't cramp. She didn't even twitch. Just stayed exactly as she was, her soft, warm body snuggled up to him.

Alexis Worthington had turned out to be the biggest surprise he'd had in a long time. Not just in bed. He remembered the stuffy suit and ugly hairstyle when he'd first seen her, and decided right then she wasn't worth a second look. Damn, he'd been wrong.

He'd thought she was all starch and no give, but hell, she hadn't complained about a thing. Not about the motel, the trailer, the less-than-stellar rest stops, none of it.

Some spoiled rich kid she'd turned out to be.

Not that she didn't have her moments. It was obvious she liked fine things. Her purse and shoes alone had to be worth more than Betsy. Throw in the gold Rolex and he supposed it would cover his truck, too. Lucky for him she'd been sent to get him, or he would never have met someone like her. Though why she'd come in person, or how she'd pissed off her father remained mysteries. Something told him the two things were related.

Her lashes fluttered. She moved closer, moaning quietly. Not a good moan, more a sound of distress. He remained still, waiting, watching. She shifted away, and moaned again.

"Lexy?"

She frowned, then opened her eyes. Her gaze swept the room before landing on his face, and she smiled. "Is it morning?"

"I think so. You were moaning."

"Oh." She stretched out her legs and winced. "It's nothing. Muscles I haven't used in a while. That's all. What time is it?"

He couldn't help a grin as he strained to see the clock. None of his business which muscles she had or hadn't been using lately, but he could still be pleased. He held her tighter when she tried to give him room. "It's five-fifteen. Go back to sleep."

A small smile tugged at her lips. "Are you going to sleep?"

"Depends on what that smile is for."

"Mmm, guess."

He felt her nipples hardening against his chest. His cock had been half-hard since he'd woken up. "What about those sore muscles?"

"You of all people should know about getting right back on the horse." Her thumb started doing those tiny circles on his belly that worked like an On switch.

"You do remember we don't have another condom," he said, sliding down so that he could kiss her neck, zeroing in on the spot that prompted all kinds of wiggling and whimpering.

She shivered. "That didn't stop us from getting creative last night."

The light rasp of his beard against her skin cooled him off. He drew back and used his tongue to soothe the afflicted area. "How about I get dressed, go to my trailer and shave, then bring back some condoms?"

"This doesn't bother me," she said, cupping her hand to his jaw. "I kind of like it."

"You won't for long." He turned his head and kissed her palm. "I've already left a mark." He touched the red spot on the side of her neck, then pushed his fingers into her hair.

"I can't feel it."

"After I get through with you, you will."

Her response was something between a laugh and a sexy moan. She closed her eyes when he started to massage her scalp. Her hand slid down his chest, over his belly. In a minute it would be hell trying to force himself to put on clothes. Or think.

"Let's stay another night," he murmured the moment she wrapped her hand around his cock. It leaped at her touch, which unfortunately slackened.

"We can't." She moved her hand away altogether. "You know we can't."

"Why not? We'll still make it to Houston in plenty of time."

"Why take the chance? Anything could happen to delay us."

Although he still had his arm around her, she'd shifted so that she was lying on her back and staring at the ceiling. "You should go back to sleep. You have a lot of driving to do today."

"What just happened?"

Briefly closing her eyes, she took a deep breath, her bare breasts rising and falling with the effort. She tried to pull up the covers, but he caught her hand.

"Lexy, come on."

"I'm cold."

"No, you aren't." He curled the arm she was lying on and

brought her warm body back to him. "Looks as if you're starting to regret last night."

"No." She met his gaze, only for an instant, then laid her cheek on his chest. "I swear to you I have no regrets, not about last night. But we still have to get to Houston."

"And?"

"I know you don't think I've behaved unprofessionally but the fact remains, I'm here on business."

"This is about your father, isn't it?"

Her head came up. She gave him an icy glare. Then her shoulders slumped. "To some degree, yes. He heads the company. If he found out, he'd—" She closed her eyes briefly, then opened them and studied him with enough caution to make him itch. "I told you I'd upset him, and we've been on rocky ground ever since. It's been ten years."

"Ten?" He couldn't hide his shock. Ten years ago she'd been a kid.

She got up on one elbow. "It started when I refused to go to Harvard. I'd secretly applied to Stanford, was accepted and told him that's where I was going."

"I didn't go to college, but I know Stanford isn't exactly a hole in the wall."

"No," Lexy agreed. "But my father's a Harvard man, so are my brother and grandfather and all his brothers."

"What about the women? You gotta have some of those in your family." He smiled. "Besides you."

She smiled back. "Most of them got a pass. They weren't directly involved with the company. Their jobs were to give dinner parties, make intelligent conversation and babies." Sighing, she picked at a thread from the pillowcase. "I could've just gone to Harvard to make him happy but the whole thing got out of control. I expected him to give in. But instead, he started finding fault with everything I did, from the boys I dated to the clothes I wore. Which made me angrier and more rebellious. I sure never expected him to cut me out of everything."

Tanner frowned. "Like disown you?"

"No, nothing like that. I went home for holidays and we saw each other at social events." She shrugged. "We were civil. But when it came to paying for school or pretty much anything, I was on my own."

He let out a low whistle. "Stanford had to be a bite in the ass. My brother only went to a Texas university and it wasn't cheap. Law school nearly gave me a heart attack."

"Your mom had died..." She tilted her head to the side and studied him. He knew what was coming next and wished he'd been more careful with his words. "Did you pay your brother's tuition?"

"Doug was still a kid." He scrubbed at his face. Much as he hated talking about it, he didn't want to be a jackass. She'd just confided more in him than she probably did most people. "He couldn't make that kind of money while he was in school. I didn't want him starting out in life with a huge debt on his back."

A soft smile lifted the corners of Lexy's mouth. She leaned over and kissed him. "You are incredibly sweet."

"Ah, Jesus." Why did she have to ruin such a nice kiss? "Are you blushing?"

"Hell, no."

She laughed. "Too bad. You *are* a sweet brother. Mine couldn't wait to fill my shoes." Her mouth tightened and she stared down at her hand. "To be fair to Harrison, I hadn't realized how much my father had favored me. For years it seemed I could do no wrong, then all of a sudden I could do absolutely nothing right. Maybe it was a lesson I was meant to learn. Harrison never deserved to be treated like second best."

"He's younger?"

"A year older."

Tanner already didn't like the guy. "He should've been looking out for you."

Shaking her head, she said, "It can't be easy living in a sibling's shadow. As I'm now finding out." She let out a startled laugh, as if the thought had just occurred to her. "Oh, well, Harrison has secured his corner of the empire. I've done my groveling. I imagine I'll be given a few more absurd errands like this—" She jerked a look at him. "Nothing personal, so don't take offense."

"None taken."

She ran her gaze down his chest to his poor, ignored cock. "On the other hand, this trip turned out to be a bonus." She moved closer, pressing her lips to the side of his ribs, then lower, until his cock started gearing up for the party.

He stopped her. It about killed him, but he didn't know if he'd have another chance at a heart-to-heart. "How did you end up paying for school?"

"Really?" She slid an inch lower and looked up at him through her lashes. "You still want to talk?"

"That's just— Oh, man." He tensed at the feel of her tongue on his belly, and stopped her.

Watching him jerk the sheet over his hips, Lexy let out a short laugh. "Seriously?"

"It's not like I'm thrilled about this."

"Well…"

He blocked her. "Lord, give me strength," he said to the ceiling. To her he said, "Now talk."

She sank back against her pillow. "I had some money stashed, did some tutoring, I even managed to qualify for scholarship and grant money. I felt horrible when so many kids needed it but I honestly didn't know what else to do. I'm going to find a way to replace every penny when I can touch my trust fund. For now, though, my salary, whatever that ends up being, will go toward student loans and credit-card balances." She caught his surprise. "Yes, by junior year

I had to apply for student loans, which also helped cover graduate school. I made enough from working part-time for living expenses and books, but that's all."

Tanner didn't know what to make of what she was telling him. Hard to believe her family could've been that cold. But then all he had to do was think of his own father, the worthless bum. He'd had no trouble turning his back on his own blood. "What about your mom, your grandparents? No one stepped in to help you?"

She pressed her lips together, and for a moment he wished he hadn't asked the question. The sadness in her eyes sliced clean through him. "I thought—" She stopped to clear her throat. "The truth is I kept hoping my mom or my grandmother would've come to my rescue, but apparently, they agreed with him. Or didn't want to interfere."

"Your mom? She's supposed to—" He cut himself off but it was too late. He didn't even know where this sudden feeling of protectiveness had come from, but she didn't need him stating the obvious. "Hey, it happens. My own father is useless to the bone."

The hurt faded from her expression. Questions swirled in her eyes. He figured she'd ask them at some point.

"It's okay. Really. I imagine they disapproved of my behavior at times and considered me an embarrassment." She looked at him, obviously read his doubt, and broke out in a huge grin. "Hey, when I do something, I go all out. My rebellion reached impressive levels. Just don't research me on Google from my college days." She paused, concern flickering in her face. "Seriously, don't."

He tried not to smile. That pretty much sealed the deal. He was getting himself an iPad.

"On the upside, the past few years have been a valuable learning experience. I found out that I come by my stubborn pride honestly." She gave a small rueful smile. "Discovered what it felt like to be poor, that yes, I can actually cook if

I'm hungry enough. And amazingly, I will not languish in obscurity just because I haven't updated my wardrobe with the *It* color of the season." She got up on her knees. "And by the way, I can unequivocally say, being rich is immeasurably better." Placing her hands on his shoulders, she swung a leg over him.

Immediately, he forgot most of what she'd just said. He let his head fall back, gripping her bare waist while she straddled him. Tough decision, looking into her eyes and waiting for her kiss, or burying his face in her soft, round breasts. The sheet served as a barrier between them, arguably a good thing. It was probably smart to leave it be, though smart wasn't cutting it for him at the moment.

"So, where were we before all this stupid talk?" she asked, leaning in so that her nipples grazed his chest and her lips brushed his, then she sat back to smile at him.

With a quiet growl of frustration, he plucked at the cheap cotton in protest.

"Poor baby," she said, petting him. "I know it's hard." The word had barely left her mouth and she laughed. "No pun intended. Hey, are you pouting?"

Tanner wasn't happy but he wasn't a pouter, either. Giving her backside a light pat, he surged up and gave her a quick kiss. "I'm going to get the condoms."

"Wait." She pushed his shoulders back against the headboard, then slowly raked her fingers through his hair. "Thank you."

"For what?"

"For listening." She pressed a kiss on his lips. "For not judging." Then planted one below his ear, the same spot she liked being kissed. It felt good. "For wanting to defend me."

He cradled her face in his hands. He believed everything she'd told him. It wouldn't surprise him if she ended up doing more than just return the grant money. "I don't know what kind of person you were before…but I sure admire who you are now."

"Oh, Tanner." She held on to his wrists and they both leaned in at the same time, bumping noses and laughing. "I'm going to make a pit stop, then dump out my makeup bag just in case I overlooked a condom. Will you stay right here?"

He rubbed his prickly jaw. "I should shave…"

"No, stay here. Promise."

Nodding, he watched her dismount and then walk naked to the bathroom. The view alone was enough to keep him stock-still. "Lexy?"

She turned with a sweet smile on her lips.

"We're gonna get to Houston on time. You'll meet your deadline, I can promise you that."

"I know." She looked as if she wanted to crawl back into bed with him, and he wouldn't have minded one bit. But then she sighed and disappeared behind the bathroom door.

As soon as it closed, he let out a breath he hadn't known was trapped in his chest. Lexy was different. He couldn't think of a woman he knew who was anything like her. The thought made him a little uneasy. No good would come of him getting too attached to her. They lived in different worlds. Always would. He did all right financially. At least he'd been smart enough to invest most of his winnings. But he couldn't afford to keep someone like her happy.

And why the hell was he even thinking about that kind of crap? Jesus. They'd had dinner and sex. And yeah, some intense conversation. So what?

He thought he heard his phone ring and turned to the clock. Too early for anyone to be calling. Course everyone who had his number knew they had to leave a message most of the time. The idea that it could be Doug had him jumping off the bed and diving for his jeans.

"Will, is that you?"

He frowned at the unfamiliar voice. "Yeah, it's Tanner."

"This is Archie Crawford. Remember me? Hank and Elizabeth's neighbor?"

"Sure, Mr. Crawford." He hadn't seen the old geezer in years. The guy had to be close to ninety, half of his life spent living to Pop and… His heart slammed his chest. "Is everything okay?"

"No, Will, it ain't. I'm guessin' you don't know about what's happening to your grandparents' ranch because if you did, you woulda stopped it."

"Mr. Crawford, please, first tell me they're all right."

"That depends, son. If you call having their ranch pulled out from under them being all right."

"What?" He paced to the window. No use getting mad at the old man. Even if he was slower than molasses getting to the point. "Who's trying to take their ranch?"

"The government, that's who. Auctioning off the whole enchilada for back taxes. Used to be they watched out for us elderly folk. No more. Now those bloodsuckers swoop in and take what they want."

It didn't make sense. If Pop and Nana needed money for taxes they would've told him. "Are you sure about this?"

"Dang tootin', I'm sure. The auction signs have already gone up."

"When?" He glanced at the closed bathroom door and lowered his voice. "When's the auction?"

"Two days from now, maybe three."

Tanner closed his eyes and cursed under his breath. He looked toward the bathroom. Lexy was not going to like this. Houston was gonna have to wait.

12

By the time Lexy walked out of the bathroom, Tanner was pulling on his shirt. That she was empty-handed was a relief. He'd hate to think a condom would undermine his resolve, but he preferred not to be tested.

She met his gaze, her eyes wide with surprise. "I thought I heard your phone. What's going on?"

She was still naked, the sight of her tempting curves forcing him to ignore the shirt snaps and go to her. He put his arms around her and held her close. The rousing sensation of her breasts pillowed against his bare chest almost made him forget what he had to do.

Briefly shutting his eyes, he ordered himself to look at her. This would be hard, but being a coward would make the situation worse. Leaning back he stared at her soft smile, and a warmth far more dangerous than lust heated his body.

No, he couldn't look at her.

He drew her again into the circle of his arms and kissed her hair. "I hate those sheets," he said. At least that wasn't a lie. "And since I need to shave and shower, anyway, I was thinking that it would be better to pack up and get on the road. That way we can stop early and find a nicer motel."

She hadn't moved, yet somehow her body seemed to have stiffened.

"Maybe even stay at one of those fancy hotels with a big Jacuzzi in the bathroom." He rubbed her back, kissed the curve of her neck. "What do you think?"

"This has something to do with that phone call, doesn't it?" she said, pulling away to look at him.

He sighed. "Yes and no."

Her brows rose expectantly. When he didn't elaborate, she started gathering her clothes.

"I have some family business to take care of," he said. "It'll require a few phone calls that I can make on the way to the trailer, then— Why do you seem disappointed? I figured you'd like a nicer room."

She slipped into her blouse, no bra, then held the jeans in front of her. "I have the feeling there's more to it." She searched his face, a trace of hurt and confusion in her eyes. "Look, if you regret what happened last night, I can't do anything about that, really. But I'd appreciate you keeping it between us. Things could be bad for me if…"

Tanner sighed. "Come here." He ended up going to her. "I don't regret last night. I wish we could stay in bed for a week," he said, running his hands up and down her arms, relieved when a small smile formed on her lips. "Hey, I'm willing to give it a go if you wanna skip Houston."

She made a face. "Nice try."

"Well, then how about after Houston?"

Lexy had that soft expression again, reminding him that he'd better think about what he was saying. It wasn't as if he'd pegged her for the clingy type. If anything, she'd likely be ready to walk away as quickly as he would. Maybe quicker. And he didn't need that heartache.

"So what do you say? Shall we pack up, get on the road?" He brushed a kiss across her lips. "We can stop for breakfast later and you can look up hotels on your phone."

"Wow, you know I can do that? You're getting so tech savvy."

"Ah, so funny." He gave her butt a squeeze. "I gotta get with the program and learn how to look up your wild college days."

The teasing smile disappeared. "Tanner."

He chuckled. "After I get showered and unhook the trailer I'll come by for you."

"While towing Betsy? Wouldn't it be easier if I walk over with my bag?"

He didn't know why her referring to the trailer by name pleased him, but it did. He just looked at her, wondering if he was wrong to not tell her what was going on. Even with a detour to West Texas, they'd still make it to Houston in time. She might worry, but he could convince her it would work out.

On the other hand, he hadn't talked to his grandparents yet. For all he knew, Archie Crawford was senile. It didn't make sense the taxes had gone unpaid. He gave Pop and Nana money twice a year even though they objected every time. It was probably nothing. Tanner would call Pop and clear everything up.

"It's not a difficult question," she said, frowning at him until he almost admitted he'd lost track of their conversation. "Look, I'll meet you over there."

Oh, right. "But your bag."

"I'll call for a luggage attendant."

"What?"

"It was a joke. I can handle my own bag." She shook her head. "Go. I'll see you when I see you."

"All right." He cupped his hand around her nape and held her still for a kiss. She parted her lips, arching against him and getting his cock far too involved.

She broke contact first. "Where's your belt?"

He found it on the floor, then finished buttoning his shirt. She practically shoved him out the door, which was just as well. As soon as he hit the parking lot he checked the time and did the math. Texas was two hours ahead. Pop and Nana would be awake by now. He hit speed dial and didn't like that no one answered. But at least he hadn't gotten a disconnect recording.

While crossing the street he tried his brother. Again no answer so he left a message. Though if Doug had known anything, he would've said. Tanner still wanted to talk to him in case it became a legal matter.

If the ranch really was being auctioned off, it was possible his grandparents had left the house and he wouldn't be able to reach them. He'd hate to call the county to see what was what, but he would. Man, he couldn't even think of the small spread belonging to anyone else. Pop and Nana loved that rickety old ranch. And it was still home for Doug and him, even though Doug lived in Dallas now. Their mother had been born in the modest brick house.

He refused to think about that stuff now. As far as explaining to Lexy, there was still too much he didn't know yet. In all likelihood this was nothing but a false alarm. It would only frustrate him if she asked questions he couldn't answer. Or if she got nervous about making it to Houston on time. And to be honest, pride was involved. He'd hate for her to think he was such a shitty grandson that they hadn't come to him.

For now all he could do was wait for calls to be returned and get on the road as quickly as possible in case they had to make a detour.

A COUPLE HOURS into the drive Lexy started to doze. She jerked and brought her head up. Tanner reached for her hand and smiled when she looked over at him.

"Try to sleep," he said. "You need the rest. That's why I'm leaving the radio low."

She stared at his tanned, much bigger hand dwarfing hers. It was weird to have a guy hold her hand. She wasn't used to it, not since high school, anyway, but it was kind of nice.

Okay, very nice. Definitely more intimate than she'd imagined, and completely unexpected. The act seemed oddly sentimental, and she didn't think Tanner was the type.

"I don't need much sleep," she said. "I should be driving so you can nap. Betsy shouldn't be a problem as long as I don't have to reverse."

"I plan on keeping you up until the wee hours, so you'd better think twice about grabbing some shut-eye."

"You're the one who might have trouble staying up tonight," she said, sweeping a gaze down his front.

He snorted a laugh. "Think so?" His hand moved up her arm toward her breast.

"Hey." She shrunk toward her door but he had a long reach. "Concentrate on driving. And look for a place to stop for breakfast. I'm starved— Oh, dammit." She stomped her foot. "I forgot my leftover steak and the cobbler."

"Calm down. I won't let you go hungry."

"I know, but I still hate wasting food." She folded her arms across her chest, aware of the curious look he'd given her. Her frugalness still surprised her, that and how conscious she'd become of not wasting anything. In the beginning she'd resented having to stretch every dollar, make the most of a bag of groceries. She couldn't say she was thrilled about it now, but she did appreciate knowing how to survive on so little.

"Why did it take you this long to hit up your father for a job?"

"I don't think of it that way. The company is a family business. I have a right to be there."

"Guess I could've phrased that better."

"No." She sighed. "I'm being touchy."

"See…not enough sleep."

"Wrong. I've adapted to getting very little sleep and I do fine."

"Staring at the ceiling and worrying about bills?"

She practically glared at his profile. She'd told him a lot, but she'd never said anything about that.

He kept his attention on the road. "Hey, we've all been there at one time or another."

Not the Worthingtons, except for her. "Pride," she said finally. "Pride kept me from going to him. And for a while I did have a job. Nothing great, but I was lucky to find anything. People took one look at my last name and couldn't believe I needed the work. Probably thought I was a corporate spy."

"What happened to the job?"

"I got laid off. Until then I'd made enough to break even every month so I would've stuck with it." She hadn't shaken the feeling her father may have had something to do with her sudden pink slip. But she had no proof. A sign for an upcoming exit caught her attention. "If you're not hungry yet, I can wait, but I'd like more coffee."

His gaze went to the dashboard clock. "Sure," he said readily enough, but he wasn't himself. Not since the phone call. "We can get breakfast. I think there's a pancake house coming up. Sound good?"

"I could handle a few pancakes." She hesitated. "We can turn the radio off if you're worried about hearing your phone."

"I have the volume turned up." He glanced over at her. "I'm waiting for Doug to call. Not about the contract. It's something else."

"I know. Family stuff." God, could she be more obvious? She was nosy as hell, and that simply wasn't like her. "Look—"

"It's about my grandparents," he said, cutting her off. "I don't want you to think it has anything to do with Houston."

"I was about to tell you I'm really not fishing." She saw the corner of his mouth quirk up slightly. "I didn't say I wasn't curious."

Tanner smiled. "I'll have to make a call when we stop. There's a mix-up with the property tax on their ranch. I've been waiting for the county office to open so I can straighten out the problem."

"You're such a good grandson."

His mouth tightened. How he could've found fault with that comment was beyond her. He opened a compartment above the rearview mirror, got out his sunglasses and slipped them on. Probably to hide behind the dark lenses.

Lexy laid her head back and tried not to be bothered by his silence. The fact that she'd told him so much about her life meant nothing. She'd volunteered. He'd asked several questions, but he hadn't pried. And to be fair, she hadn't really asked him anything. No reason for him to reciprocate. Screw it. She had a few questions of her own. Up to him if he chose to answer.

"Are they your mother's parents?"

He seemed startled by the casual query, hesitating before he nodded. "She was their only daughter. So Doug and I are the only grandkids. We're all close."

"What about your father? Does he still have contact with them?"

Tanner's grip on the wheel tightened as he steered the truck off the exit ramp, his face full of contempt. "He doesn't give a damn about anyone but himself. The only thing that bastard has ever done right is feel guilty that he took her from us."

She blinked. "Are you saying he was responsible for your mother's death?"

"As if he'd pulled the trigger himself." He was back in control, nearly devoid of expression.

"I'm sorry for bringing it up." *Trigger?* Had his mother

been murdered? Wishing they'd stayed on the expressway, Lexy held a hand to her suddenly queasy stomach. She no longer wanted coffee or food.

He looked over, dividing his attention between her and the road. "It's okay. I get worked up sometimes, but hey, it happened a long time ago."

"This isn't about me," she said, evading him when he tried to take her hand. "You're allowed to feel anything you want, but you also have to drive."

At that moment the truck weaved a little. Tanner quickly brought it to rights. Fortunately, they'd reached a strip mall with a gas station at one end and the pancake house on the other. He turned the truck into the parking lot and found a stall.

As soon as he cut the engine, he angled his body toward her. "I might've given you the wrong idea. My mom died in the Gulf War," he said, taking off his sunglasses and tossing them on the dash. "She enlisted as a reservist without telling anyone. She did it for the extra money. I was too young to know what was going on but according to my grandfather she didn't think she'd ever be deployed.

"I know it sounds bad. Unpatriotic and all that." Shrugging, he swung a look out the windshield. "But she was desperate. They were still married…she never would've divorced him, but he came and went as he pleased. He used to be a bareback rider, a pretty good one from what I've heard, but he got injured just when he'd started winning decent money the family could live on.

"He should've quit rodeoing and gotten a job. I was eight and Doug had just turned two. But he couldn't let go. He couldn't ride anymore, but he stayed with the circuit, picked up odd jobs, sent home a few bucks now and then. Showed up for holidays or when he didn't have enough money to get to the next event."

After a sizeable stretch of silence, Lexy asked, "Is he the reason you're a bareback rider?"

"Hell, no." He turned back to her with a look of such derision, a chill slithered down her spine. "If anything I ended up rodeoing in spite of him. I was good at it, didn't like school all that much and I knew I had a shot at making more money riding than I could at anything else." Tanner settled back into neutral. "Doug's smart and he wanted to go to college. My grandparents barely made enough from the ranch to keep up with two growing boys. There was no money for a good school. Any school," he murmured, his voice dropping off.

"Stop it." She took his hand, and he stared at her with a confused frown. "You don't have to defend your choices. You not only stepped up, but you've been an incredible role model for your brother. I'd bet you've helped your grandparents, too."

He yanked his hand away. "I told you before, I'm no saint. So don't go painting pretty pictures in your head."

No, he wasn't a saint, but he was a damn good man. Lexy pressed her lips together as if that would ease the burning behind her eyes. She stared down at her lap, shame coming at her in waves. "You must think I'm the worst human being ever born. I feel like a complete tool complaining to you about my life."

He nudged her chin up. "That's the thing. You don't complain. You haven't on this trip." His expression softened. "I had trouble believing you were a rich heiress."

"Oh, trust me, I can be a real princess."

Tanner smiled. "Yeah, I've caught a few glimpses of the tiara."

"I have news for you. I do complain. In my head, I complain a lot. And do my share of swearing, too." She blinked, relieved the dreaded tears hadn't welled. "Tiara? Really?"

The skin at the corner of his eyes crinkled. "Man, I must

be crazy, too much time out in the sun maybe, but here's some real-time truth. Just figured it out myself. I think I did end up rodeoing because of the old man. From the time I was three I used to jump on anything that moved and tried to ride it."

"Oh." Lexy let out a soft gasp. "That could've been dangerous."

"I got yelled at real good when I hopped on the chainsaw Pop left leaning against the woodpile. That's my granddad, and of course the chainsaw wasn't going."

"Ooh." She winced.

"Yeah." He faked a shudder, then turned his head, his smile fading as he stared off. "The old man used to let me ride on his back while he pretended to be a horse. When I got older, he put me on my first pony. I think I was trying to get his attention. Make him proud of me so he'd stay home and we'd be a normal family." Tanner smiled at her again. "So I'll let him have that one. He's partly responsible for my being here."

It seemed every time he spoke, she admired him more. "I don't know anyone like you," she whispered.

"Ditto."

When he leaned toward her, she did, too, until their lips met. The kiss was gentle and very satisfying.

She moved her head back. "May I ask another question?"

"Shoot."

"Do you know where he is now?"

"Yeah, he's still around. Chasing the tour like always." Tanner took off his hat. "I run into him sometimes and I'm civil enough. He's only in his early fifties but he looks like shit. Probably guilt. Good."

She smiled a little, and so did Tanner. He wasn't quite as hard-nosed as he pretended to be regarding his father. She had no illusions. He probably still suffered from bouts of anger and resentment. She'd witnessed a trace of it earlier.

But clearly Tanner hadn't allowed bitterness to control his life. Maybe she could learn from him.

"Well, aren't we a pair? Our idiot fathers should meet sometime."

He snorted. "Ah, no, some things should be left alone." Placing his Stetson on the console between them, he said, "Let's get something to eat."

Astonishingly, she was starting to feel hunger again. "You still treating?"

"I'm running a tab."

"Don't joke about it. I want you to give me a bill and we're going to triple the total before I turn it in."

"Still want to stick it to Daddy, huh?"

"Yes." She opened the door and slid out of the truck. "Yes, I do," she said before closing the door.

In truth, she could submit a huge expense account for the trip and her father would never know. And even if he did, the extravagance wouldn't faze him. But it was fun sharing the joke with Tanner.

He held his hand out to her, and she could feel the blush move up her throat. It was so stupid. He was just being gentlemanly. Still, she felt like a young girl out on a date.

"After we order, you mind if I come out and make my call?" He held her hand as they walked to the restaurant's entrance.

"No, of course not. Make it now if you want, and I'll wait inside." Out of the corner of her eye she saw a variety store. "Or maybe you could advance me a few more bucks so I can pick up a couple of T-shirts."

He turned to follow her gaze. "I think I can handle that," he said, bringing his eyes back to her face. "For a kiss."

"Here? Now?"

"Sure."

Right in front of the crowded restaurant's windows,

Lexy threw her arms around his neck and laid a whopper on him that sent him staggering back a step.

It was hard kissing and laughing at the same time. She felt great. Better than she had in years. All because of Tanner. And that alone should've scared the hell out of her.

13

TANNER SAT IN the truck at a rest stop, watching for Lexy to come out of the bathroom while talking to his brother, who'd known nothing about the auction. "You sure about this?"

"I could be wrong but I don't think so," Doug said. He sounded worried, which didn't help Tanner's optimism. "I don't like that no one from the county called you back."

"Is it a government holiday or something?" He'd left two detailed messages offering to pay the taxes, penalties, anything they wanted. "You'd think they'd be dialing with one hand and holding out the other one."

"It may be too late to pay the taxes. Once the wheels are in motion, the bureaucracy goes full speed ahead. Crawford say how many years Pop and Nana were behind?"

"No, and I didn't ask." Frustrated, Tanner pushed a hand through his hair. "Jesus, I wish I could talk to *somebody*. I guess the next step is to pull out some of my investments."

"Not yet. We don't even know if any of this is true."

"I hope it isn't, but I have to be prepared to bid if it comes to that. We could find out the auction is day after tomorrow. I don't have a lot of cash lying around."

After a long pause, Doug said, "Man, I hate that you have to do that. I have maybe four grand in my office account, another thousand in my checking." He let out a string of curses. As a teenager Tanner had taught him every one of them. He wasn't feeling too proud. "I had no business taking this damn vacation."

"Knock that shit off. Nobody could've seen this coming. You never take time away. And don't cut your trip short. Can't you handle everything by phone?" He straightened when he saw Lexy leave the building. "Too late to make calls now, but tomorrow?"

"If there's an auction, I should go with you. It's not fair that you always do the heavy lifting. I'm not a kid anymore."

"Don't switch your flight yet. Look, I gotta go."

"Call me later."

"Yep." He disconnected and checked the bars on the phone. Only one. He had to remember to charge the damn thing. And he'd better figure out how he'd break the news to Lexy if it turned out Crawford was right. Houston was east and as far south as you could get and still be in Texas. The ranch was located to the west, past Hill Country. By tomorrow they'd have to change course.

"Did you find a hotel?" she asked as soon as she climbed in.

"Nope. I'm leaving that job to you. I was talking to Doug."

"Oh." She paused as he reversed the truck. "You know I don't mind sleeping in the trailer."

"I don't have a tub back there." He was tempted to take her up on the offer. They could keep driving instead of looking for a nice motel that was suitable both for Lexy and for parking a trailer. But they'd made great time, having already crossed into Colorado, and getting to West Texas wasn't the issue. Depending on when the auction was held, driving from there to Houston could be the problem.

"You look tired." She reached over and stroked his

beard-roughened jaw. "I say we stop at the first place that can accommodate Betsy."

Her touch settled it. He was still running on adrenaline but that would die out as soon as they hunkered down for the night. "You better be sure. I know a park about forty miles from here."

"You have a bed back there, don't you?" she said, moving her hand to his thigh. More interested in where her hand would end up, he gave her a vague nod. She grinned. "Then I'm sure."

Within an hour they'd arrived at the park and hooked up Betsy under the shade of an old poplar tree. Then they'd snacked on crackers, cheese and fruit…Lexy's choice. He'd offered her a restaurant dinner that she'd turned down. Though she hadn't said, he was pretty sure it was because she thought he was beat. No one had worried about him like that in a while. It felt nice, but at the same time, risky.

Another downside to Betsy…the shower was small. Didn't stop them from trying to get in there together. Tanner finally gave up when he saw they were headed for a world of hurt. Tanner let Lexy go first, and after he was finished with his turn, he found her in the kitchen wearing his blue shirt and studying the pictures taped to the fridge.

She heard him and turned, her gaze going straight to the towel wrapped around his hips. Her face lit up with a smile. "Good. Just the way I want you."

"I'll take you any way I can get you."

He slid his arms around her, and she leaned back against his chest.

"Have you decided yet?" she asked, gasping softly when he reached underneath the shirt to cup her breast.

He stared over her shoulder at the pictures. He understood the question. Earlier he'd told her how much grief the guys gave him over trying to decide between retiring to the mountains or the beach. "Nope."

"They're fading. When did you put these up?"

"Don't recall."

She moved her hips, rubbing her ass against his hard-on. "This is a joke, isn't it? You aren't really going to spend the rest of your life fishing."

"I might."

"I don't believe you. Neither of these places suits you and that's why I think you put these pictures up. You don't have to give it serious thought because you won't choose either one. You just like messing with people."

"Is that right?"

"Oh." She let her head loll back when he nuzzled her neck, then made that soft, breathy sound he loved. "Have you even been to—?"

"Stop—" he turned her to face him "—talking," he said, and came down on her mouth a little too rough. Making it up to her, he soothed her soft lips with his tongue. He found the first snap, and with a slight jerk heard two pops, leaving the shirt hanging open. "I like this," he murmured against her mouth. "Feel free to wear my clothes anytime."

"Wanna talk or test your sheets?" She bubbled with laughter, and broke for the back of the trailer. The shirt fell from her shoulders before she hit the bed.

He watched her slide that curvy naked body up to the pillows, worried that he'd come before he lost the damn towel. Leaving it on the floor, he crawled in behind her. And managed to take a nip of her butt before she turned onto her back.

LEXY JERKED AT the unexpected scrape of his teeth on her skin. As soon as she flipped over, he used her surprise to spread her thighs. He kissed inside the left one, then stroked his tongue intimately up her fold. Inspiring another gasp, he parted her moist flesh and took another swipe with his tongue.

She whimpered when he stopped too soon, but he kept going up her stomach, leaving a wet trail to her belly button, then circling it before licking his way to her breasts and sucking a nipple into his mouth. She was about to explode. Shuddering deep inside, she closed her eyes, unable to move by the time he got to her mouth.

A fiery sensation ignited low in her belly, and she knew it was time to bring out a condom. She slapped blindly at the small table beside the bed. The box hit the floor. For all his restraint, Tanner seemed just as eager and quickly retrieved it. He dug out a packet, tore it open and sheathed himself.

He slowed down long enough to kiss her lips, brush the hair from her face and look into her eyes. Already positioned between her thighs, he pulled her legs around his waist and pushed into her, his muscled arms trembling.

"I know this will go fast, but I don't care," she murmured, moving her hips, urging him not to hold back. "I want you."

He drew back slightly, then thrust into her. The bed shook. A growl tore from his throat the whole park could probably hear. She wasn't quiet, either. Didn't even try to cover her mouth. Her right hand fisted the sheets. With the other, she clutched his muscled arm. Her fingernails were digging into him but she couldn't seem to let go. She bucked up to meet his second thrust, and then his third. With the fourth, the bed seemed to spin beneath her.

She flushed feverishly hot, then went shivery cold. His body tensed, his arm muscles bunching rock-hard so that her nails lost traction. Helpless but to release him, she fell back as the spasms gripped her, pulling her into an unrelenting undertow of sensations.

Tanner stilled, muscles taut and straining as he came. His long, low moan sounded otherworldly, hot, sexy as anything she'd ever heard. He looked beautiful. His body tanned and rugged and virile.

Her climax hadn't eased. The pressure seemed to impossibly build again, regaining momentum, then crashing over her, blurring her vision and overwhelming her senses. Adrift once more, she came around and realized his circling thumb was the reason. She shifted her legs to the side, breaking contact, and he collapsed beside her.

But the best part? The most perfect thing ever…Tanner had never stopped looking into her eyes.

BY NINE THE next morning they'd eaten breakfast and were on the road again. Lexy leaned as far back as the passenger seat allowed, stretched out her legs and started a second round of yawning.

"You slept well last night," Tanner said, hoping he hadn't rushed her. Not knowing more details about the auction was maddening. He figured he'd get there in time, but he also wanted to make good on his promise to Lexy of a nice hotel, an early check-in and lots of lovemaking. "Can't tell me otherwise."

She set her to-go mug of coffee down, and he knew what that meant. "Are you implying that I snore?"

"Don't you dare tickle me while I'm driving. I mean it."

"Oh, okay," she said, and he glanced over and caught her sly grin. "Since you mean it, that changes everything."

"Such gorgeous blue eyes. Who knew you could be so ruthless?" Damn, she'd found that one tiny spot near his butt…his fault for reacting, but she hadn't let up, either.

"You're right. No tickling now. But later? I make no promises." She picked up her coffee. "I don't snore. Do I?"

"No. But you did hit the pillow hard."

"I know. It's weird. For a year nothing has helped my insomnia. But the last two nights with you I've fallen asleep in minutes."

"I'll try not to take that wrong."

"Oh, come on. I'm not falling for that crap."

"What?" he asked, laughing at her inelegant snort.

"You're like a pool hustler."

"Not my game."

"You know what I mean. Preying on unsuspecting women, unleashing that charm of yours until they're too weak to resist."

He gave her a long look. "Jesus, you win. Go back to sleep."

"I know," she said, laughing at herself. After pausing a moment she asked, "Why aren't you married?"

"Odd question. Can't imagine I seem the type."

"But you do. Even though you spend so much time on the road…" She trailed off. "Let me reword… Why aren't you in a steady relationship?"

"I tried that once. Didn't take."

Lexy hesitated. "Can I ask for how long and why?"

"We met at a rodeo and hit it off. We both liked horses and the quiet life, held similar values…" He blew out a stream of air, mulling over what he'd be comfortable sharing. "Doreen worked as a court reporter in Dallas. She understood the rodeo kept me on the road. Sometimes she'd join me for a long weekend, or I'd spend downtime with her in Dallas. I wasn't crazy about staying in the city, but we seemed to make things work for almost two years. I'll admit, marriage crossed my mind."

A gust of wind buffeted the truck and trailer. He gripped the wheel with both hands to maintain control. Lousy timing, he thought, when Lexy swung him an abrupt look. He didn't want her confusing the interruption and think he was stalling. Doreen was in the past. He rarely thought about her.

"Anyway," he continued before she prompted him. "There's not much more to the story. Doreen hated the term buckle bunny, but basically she fit the bill. I had no problem with that, but all of a sudden she started getting jealous and questioning me when I was away. Twice she accused me of sleeping with other women, meaning buckle bunnies. Never happened. I don't do that crap. If I make a commitment, I keep it."

He almost glanced at Lexy, but kept his attention in front of him. If she even vaguely looked as if she doubted him, he didn't want to know.

"Doreen would cry, tell me she was sorry and things would be okay for a while. But it finally dawned on me that she was the one cheating. Why else the sudden suspicion? I knew she'd started going to local rodeos when I was on the road. Which was fine until the crazy accusations. I couldn't prove she was screwing other riders, but I was pretty convinced."

"Did you call her on it?"

"Nope. It didn't matter at that point. If she'd really known me or loved me, there wasn't a snowball's chance in hell she would've believed I was capable of cheating."

Lexy got really quiet. Finally, he had to look at her.

She gave him a tender smile and shifted closer until her lips grazed his cheek. She kissed him, then whispered, "You're right. I've known you for only four days and I'd never believe it."

Tanner smiled.

"I'm completely serious."

The tightness in his chest was powerful enough to choke a bull. "I know you are." He wanted to thank her, but didn't trust his voice.

TANNER STOOD OUTSIDE the convenience store after fueling the truck, and waited while Lexy picked up a few things inside. He thought about trying Doug, hoping for good news, but that would be stupid. He'd only waste his brother's time. They'd already talked once and Doug was scrambling to make sure they had ready cash. If he had something new to report, he would've called. Course it wouldn't be now since the timing was perfect. Tanner was getting itchy over hiding conversations from Lexy.

After receiving no word from the county treasurer, he had placed another call to the office an hour ago. At least someone answered, an older woman with a creaky voice who'd asked him to repeat himself three times. She'd identified herself as a county clerk and confirmed the ranch was to be auctioned off in two days. Only because she'd seen the signs on the posts. In an official capacity she could tell him nothing. She'd offered to leave another message for her boss but Tanner didn't hold out much hope. He knew how those small country offices operated. The guy was probably off fishing.

Anyway, he'd already gotten the news he'd been dreading. Archie Crawford hadn't been wrong. The ranch was scheduled to be auctioned.

He peered into the store window, trying to locate Lexy. She was next in line to be checked out so he stayed where he was on the off chance Doug called, and watched her scan the selection of candy bars. An older man standing at the register turned and said something to her. Whatever it was she didn't like it, judging by the regal lift of her chin as she shifted her attention elsewhere.

Tanner smiled. Every once in a while he got a candid glimpse of the Alexis Worthington who'd grown up in that big, fancy house with a stable and tennis court, money and servants. Hard to imagine she ever could've been the spoiled-brat type. She had too much heart and grit. And he didn't buy that a person could change that much. But he still liked his Lexy better.

Shit.

He lifted his Stetson, rubbed the back of his neck then resettled the hat on his head. That sort of thinking had to stop. She wasn't his. Yeah, he liked her…quite a bit. And she liked him. So friggin' what? He liked a lot of people. Even folks who didn't believe in him like she did.

Ah, hell. There he went, overthinking again. He was out of his ever-lovin' mind if he thought she'd really meant it about knowing he wasn't a cheater. What was he supposed to have done? Call him a liar? She'd been earnest and everything, probably believed what she'd said in the moment. But the fact was, she didn't really know him. That was okay. What he needed to remember was that she never would. It was gonna be adios soon.

Maybe he should think about doing the calendar. That'd keep her in his sights a while longer. Hell, he couldn't do that, it would kill him. If he wanted to see more of her, he'd just man up and ask. Even if he didn't think he had a chance.

"Is something wrong?"

At the sound of her voice he jumped like a scared little girl.

"Sorry," she murmured, her voice muffled from behind her hand. She didn't have to hide her laugh.

"Nothing's wrong. Why?"

"It's just that you always—" she gestured vaguely "—adjust your hat when you're thinking hard or bothered by something."

"I do?"

She nodded. "And if it's something extra worrisome you rub the back of your neck, too."

"Huh." Good thing he didn't wear his hat playing poker. They fell into step heading for the truck. "What did the guy in the store want?"

She frowned for an instant. "Oh." Her chin automatically went up. "I simply peeked at the candy bars, and he told me that if I stayed away from all that nasty sugar I wouldn't have to wear baggy men's T-shirts." She glanced down at the white variety-store shirt neatly tucked in her jeans. "Can you believe that? Some nerve."

Tanner did all he could to hold in a laugh at her haughty expression. Looping an arm around her, he hugged her to his side. "He was either blind or teasing because you look mighty fine."

"I think he was kidding, but still…" A smile tugged at her lips when he dropped a kiss on her upturned face. "It was rude."

"If he wasn't thirty years my senior I'd go punch him out for you."

She batted her lashes. "You'd do that for me?"

Grinning, he opened the passenger door and waited until she was seated. "So which candy bar did you get?"

Her eyes narrowed to slits. "Snickers and Peanut M&Ms," she admitted, albeit reluctantly, then sighed. "And Reeses' cups."

"Dibs on the Snickers," he said, and shut the door. If he had a brain he'd be worried how easily she distracted him. It plain wasn't right that he could forget about his grand-parents' ranch for even a minute.

Before he slid behind the wheel she informed him that he could have only half the Snickers or he had to go buy another one. He kissed her before starting the engine, and she passed the whole bar to him. He returned it and drove to the expressway.

Fifteen minutes later his phone rang. He glanced at his hat sitting on the console, hiding the phone. Three semi-trucks had them boxed in so he didn't dare try to answer.

"Want me to see who it is?" she asked, licking choco-late off her fingers.

After hesitating, Tanner nodded.

"It's your brother," she said.

"Tell him I'll call back when I pull over."

She had to be shocked because he'd been so damn secretive about every conversation. "Hi, Doug?" She paused. "Yes, it's Lexy. Tanner's driving but he'll call back in a few." She laughed at something he said, then disconnected. "He said okeydokey."

He shot her a look. "Doug did not say that."

"No, the cashier at the convenience store did. I thought it was cute. Doug said okay."

Although he would've preferred the ease of a rest stop, Tanner took the next exit and pulled off to the shoulder as soon as he could safely do so. He'd explained early on to Lexy that he refused to talk and drive. Not completely true, and he figured she knew it had more to do with him wanting privacy. This time he'd surprise her. The auction was in two days. He had to spill the beans soon, anyway.

Staying in the truck, he hit speed dial, aware she was openly staring. "Hey," he said when Doug answered. "Tell me something good."

"Okay," his brother drawled, and Tanner knew right then there'd be a flip side. "I found out from a law school buddy that Lesser County doesn't require cash in full with a bid. Only ten percent earnest money and financials showing you're good for it."

"All right," Tanner said. "Better than I'd hoped. Wait. How would we know the amount in advance?"

"We don't."

Sighing, he rubbed the back of his neck. "Can we check past auctions and compare area real-estate prices? Do we have time?" No, he couldn't afford to screw up. "I should just pull out everything."

"Everything? What, you want to buy the whole county?"

"Okay, whatever, you know more about what we need. Just make sure it gets into my hands fast."

"Yeah, about that…" His brother hesitated. "Ready for the bad news?"

14

TANNER HAD A split second to decide if it was a mistake to stay in the truck. But he'd parked on the shoulder so there was no other safe option. "Shoot."

"It's impossible to liquidate enough of your assets in time," Doug said, and waited for Tanner to finish cussing. "But we do have a small annuity check being overnighted, which, by the way, I had to forge your signature so I could fax the request pronto."

"I don't care about penalties for early withdrawals if that's an issue."

"No, it's strictly a timing factor. Helen's pulling comps now. At least we'll have an informed estimate on that ten percent figure. Off the cuff, I'm thinking we might have enough cash to get reasonably close. Even if we have to raid piggy banks."

"Glad you can find humor in this."

"Come on, you know better. I'm just saying we'll have to empty our checking accounts but we can do this." Doug paused. "What about Alexis? You seem cozy with her. Maybe—"

"No."

"I'm talking short-term loan."

"No."

"I understand it would be hard to ask her, but are you willing to risk Pop and Nana's ranch for the sake of pride?"

"Move on, Doug." Tanner itched to punch something. He couldn't ask Lexy even if he'd wanted to. Right now he couldn't even bring himself to look at her. She was broke. And she might stay that way if he didn't get his act together. He wasn't about to let his grandparents down, but he wouldn't fail her, either. Bad enough her father was using this stupid farce to put her in her place. Tanner had vowed to make it to Houston in time and he'd keep that promise.

"I should have some figures in the next hour or two." His brother's voice dipped in defeat. "I'm assuming there's been no word from Pop or Nana."

"I haven't heard, but then I'm not expecting to." He pinched the bridge of his nose, feeling bad for being unnecessarily hard on Doug, and trying to clear his head enough to think. "Look, you're doing great. More than I could have done. Keep going." A crazy thought started to form. Maybe not so crazy. It was only eighty miles out of the way. He glanced at the dashboard clock, hunched forward and turned the key. "I might have an idea."

"What is it?"

Tanner inhaled deeply. "I'll tell you if it works," he said, then disconnected and pulled the truck into a U-turn and headed back to the expressway.

Lexy remained quiet. She did make sure his phone was safely tucked in the cup holder so it wouldn't go flying. Focusing his attention on accessing the on-ramp, he reached for her hand. It was cold. He hoped he hadn't just frightened her.

"I looked before I made that turn."

"I know," she said. "I have no problem with your driving."

Ah, hell. He could almost hear her voice saying ...*but*

you, however... Keeping his mouth shut, he waited for her to lower the boom.

"Tanner?" she said quietly. "Whatever you have going on, I hope you know that I'll help in any way I can."

Luckily, he had good reason to keep his face straight ahead as he checked mirrors and merged into traffic. He smiled and squeezed her hand then returned his to the wheel. "Thanks."

"Oh, God, you think I'm prying."

"I don't. It didn't even cross my mind. There's this auction coming up in a few days... My grandparents are involved... Doug's handling things, and he doesn't need me stepping on his toes. I have a bad habit of rushing in too soon." He wasn't lying. "I'm pushing the whole matter aside for a while, and concentrating on a surprise I have for you."

He turned his head in time to catch her slow, pleased smile. Unfortunately, he also noticed the upcoming sign for Texas via Oklahoma City. That route wasn't part of his plan but he knew the exact moment she saw it, too.

"Did you see that sign for Oklahoma City?" Her eyes lit up and she twisted around as they passed it.

"It's just telling us we're going in the right direction, that's it. We have a ways to go."

"But we're doing well time-wise, and if we stopped there, I could pick up my new credit card, get you reimbursed and swing by my apartment for more clothes. Did it say how many miles?" She picked up her phone. "Where are we exactly?"

He breathed in slow and easy, and closing a hand over her phone, stopped her from getting online. "You're going to ruin my surprise." Again, he wasn't lying. He just wasn't connecting all the dots for her.

"That's nice, really, but I need appropriate clothes. I can't show up to the photo shoot wearing a T-shirt and jeans."

"We don't have as much spare time as you might think,"

he said, the alarm in her face making his chest tight. "Because of this family thing I'm dealing with."

She blinked, nodded. Then worried her lower lip, looking as nervous as a filly facing off with a rattler.

Goddammit, he wished like hell he'd already told her about what was going on. He'd only talked to Crawford yesterday morning, even though it seemed a lifetime ago. Would she understand why he'd waited until he knew more details, that he hadn't wanted to worry her? Would she understand what he was about to do? Or would she look at him with disappointment in those beautiful eyes?

"We'll still make it to Houston in time," he said. "As far as your clothes go, we can do one of two things—have your suit laundered, or buy something at a mall."

She obviously wasn't happy with the suggestion, but gave him a stiff nod. He felt some relief doling out another piece of truth. At least he'd meant it about the surprise. He had a nice hotel in mind, one that was sure to have a jetted tub and enough amenities to keep her busy while he played some poker. And won the pants off J.D.

LEXY MISSED THE MOUNTAINS. Parts of Wyoming and northern Colorado had reminded her of western Montana, but the terrain had been flat and dry for a few hours. Which described much of Oklahoma so she should be used to it. No reason for her to be in a funk.

She needed to rally, perk up a bit. As soon as they left the expressway she saw the row of sad, dusty motels. Pressing her lips together, she suppressed a sigh. Her idea of a *nice place* diverged greatly from Tanner's. She wasn't being a snob about it. Her only issue was that given the choice, even if he had a four-star hotel in mind, she would've preferred going through Oklahoma City. It would've been on the way and solved a couple of problems for her.

The pink stucco building with the flashing vacancy sign

made her grit her teeth. She knew with a depressing certainty that Tanner would turn into the parking lot. A cosmic payback for ten miles of her snarky thoughts. But no, he kept driving. And driving.

"What are we doing? Taking the back roads to Houston?"

He turned to her with a lifted brow. "Someone's cranky. You run out of candy bars?"

"Hey…" Her phone buzzed, saving him from the tart remark she'd been about to deliver. She saw that it was Norma and answered.

"Where are you?" Norma asked by way of greeting.

"Still in Colorado, I think," Lexy said, glancing at Tanner, expecting him to confirm or deny. He did neither. "But we're not stopping in Oklahoma City, after all. I guess you can overnight my credit card to Houston."

"Listen, I'm calling to give you a heads-up," Norma said, her voice just above a whisper. "The photo shoot has been moved up a day."

"What? No." Feeling the panic well, Lexy doublechecked the date on her watch. "Why? Who decided this?"

"Your brother, of course. Why…I don't know. I found out by accident. He and Karina had a meeting with marketing about an hour ago."

"Clearly he hasn't told me yet."

"Well, he should be the one to tell you, so I'd appreciate you keeping this between us. He and Karina left the office so quickly that I worried he'd forgotten to let you know."

Or had decided to leave her hanging. No, he wouldn't do that, but Karina might. Lexy knew Norma was thinking the same thing. Then Lexy had another awful thought. "Have they found someone else?" She couldn't help glancing at Tanner. He acted as though he wasn't paying attention but she knew better.

"I don't think so…but then they couldn't proceed with

the photo shoot without having filled the last slot…" Norma's concerned voice trailed off. "I'll see what I can find out."

"Don't cause trouble for yourself." Lexy had kept Harrison informed…sort of. He knew she'd located Tanner and would escort him to Houston. "I mean it, Norma. Harrison doesn't know we're traveling by car so he probably expects us there early."

"Don't worry about me. Be safe. I'll call again later."

Lexy kept the phone to her ear long after Norma had disconnected. Nerves had her insides jumping. She didn't want to think her brother would purposely sabotage her. The thought was horrible. She had to believe what she'd told Norma. He'd expected her to arrive early. She was bound to get a call from him at any moment. Unless Norma had gotten it wrong. That was certainly possible. Though if Lexy didn't hear, she'd phone him. Just to ease her mind. That she felt compelled to double-check depressed her all over again.

Lowering the phone to her lap, she stared out the windshield. The arid, colorless landscape did nothing to improve her mood. Finally, she turned to Tanner. He shot her a concerned look.

"That was my office. You just might be off the hook."

"Meaning?"

"Don't set your hopes too high." She forced a smile. "It's possible the woman in charge of the project found someone else for the calendar."

He didn't seem as thrilled as she'd anticipated. "What does that mean for you?"

She shrugged. "I probably shouldn't have said anything yet. I won't know for sure until I hear from my brother." Still perplexed by his subdued reaction, she added, "You do understand it means they wouldn't need you, right?"

"This isn't about me," he said. "I told you straight off I'm just riding out my contract. Tell me if I'm wrong, but isn't this whole thing supposed to be your beat-down, comeuppance or whatever you wanna call it? Before they let you back in."

"That was my assumption." She sighed, glanced at her phone to make sure she'd left the ringer on. "If they're still expecting us, that means we have to hustle. They moved the photo shoot up a day."

Tanner navigated a curve in the road, then turned to scowl at her. "You're kidding?"

"No." She studied his tense shoulders and the pulse ticking like mad at his neck. "Is that a problem? I thought we were close to Texas."

"We are. Don't sweat it. We'll cross the state line in the morning."

"Maybe we should keep driving," she said, a bit on edge from the tension he was radiating. "It's still early."

He shook his head. "Gotta make this stop."

Perfect. She couldn't tell if her nerves were a result of her brother's possible subterfuge, or the fact that Tanner had told her not to sweat while that's exactly what he was doing.

THEY HADN'T NEEDED a bellman to carry up their two small bags, but Tanner had decided to go all out, spoiling Lexy. That, and she wasn't likely to take a swing at him in the elevator in front of a witness.

The doors slid open. Smiling, he gestured for her to go ahead of him and the short, cheerful fella carrying her brown designer carry-on and Tanner's ratty canvas duffel. Silly as he felt not handling his own bag, he had a much bigger problem to fret over.

Man, he'd blown it. Big time. If he'd confided in her sooner, he wouldn't have to tell her about tomorrow's detour while she was as jittery as a hooker in church. He wasn't looking forward to that little sit-down. And yet he had to keep his head clear and ready to play some serious poker tonight.

Jose, according to the bellman's nametag, led them to a door at the end of the hall, then used Tanner's card-key to open it. The room was large, flooded with sunlight and lots of beige and blue from the striped couch to the pictures hanging on the wall.

"This is the parlor and wet bar," Jose said, still smiling. "I'll show you the bedroom."

Lexy frowned at Tanner. "This is a junior suite."

"Yep. That's what the woman at the front desk said. Don't you like it?"

"But why?"

Tanner slid his Stetson off his head and smoothed the stubborn ridge in his hair. "I wanted a room with a Jacuzzi like I promised you. It was this or the big honeymoon suite."

"You didn't have to do this." She went up on her toes and briefly kissed his mouth before they followed Jose into the bedroom.

"Hey, buddy, we can take it from here." Tanner pulled a ten out of his pocket and passed it to the man.

"I can explain how to use the remotes for the television and drapes," he said, the wide, toothy grin still in place.

"No, thanks," they said at the same time, and then exchanged a small laugh.

"All right, you folks enjoy your stay. Call the front desk or the bell captain if you need anything." He bent in an odd bow and started for the door.

"Hey, wait, Jose." Tanner went after him while peeling off another ten. "Will you tell someone to send up a bottle of wine and charge it to the room?"

"My pleasure, sir." He accepted the tip. "Would that be white or red?"

Tanner blinked, and turned toward the bedroom. "Honey, what do you drink, white or red?"

Lexy appeared at the door and gave him a look. "Red."
Well, shit.

Her chilly glare warned him he'd done something wrong.
And here he'd hoped the wine would loosen her up and
she wouldn't hand him his balls once he told her about the
change in plan.

He almost shrugged when he looked at Jose, but he was
smart enough to know that would piss her off. The man
gave a discreet, understanding nod and left.

She'd disappeared into the room, and Tanner went after
her. Coming up behind her, he wrapped her in his arms.

"What?" he murmured, his lips pressed to the side of
her neck.

She turned around to face him with a laugh. "Honey,
what do you drink?" she mimicked.

"Ah, right. I'm not supposed to call you honey."

"No. You shouldn't have made it sound as if you'd just
picked me up on a street corner."

Tanner thought on it a moment, then smiled. "You might
have a point."

"Might?" She wiggled out of his arms and headed toward the bathroom. "And what's with the ten-dollar tip?
Twice! Whoever called you a cheapskate the other day is
crazy."

He followed her, caught her hand and swung her around
to face him. "If you weren't with me, I would've given him
three," he said, trying not to laugh at her mock glare.

"You would've carried your own bag."

"I'd be sleeping in the trailer."

Lexy smiled, slipped her arms around his neck and gestured with a tilt of her head. "Look."

"Nice," he said, eyeing the big, deep tub. "We can both
fit in there, and then some."

"Who'd you have in mind?"

He took a nip of her lower lip. "I told you, Alexis." He

ran the tip of his tongue over the spot where he'd used his teeth. "I'm a one-woman man."

She sighed against his mouth. "I like you, Tanner. I really do, and I didn't mean to give you a hard time about the tips. It's your money. I've heard enough of your conversation with Doug to know you're dealing with a cash-flow problem and I don't need you to impress me with expensive hotel rooms or hot tubs or anything else." She brushed her lips across his. "Anyway, it's too late. You've already impressed me."

He moved back, too abruptly, he realized when he saw the alarm in her eyes, then watched it fade as he unbuckled her belt and drew up the hem of her T-shirt. The timing was perfect to tell her about the poker game, the back taxes, the auction. Explain why Houston wasn't his first priority. She knew so much about his predicament already. It would be easy to slide in between the half-truths and prey on her sympathy.

But he just couldn't bring it up. Not right now. He'd done the math and accounted for the new twist. They could still make it to Houston, but it would be damn tight. He could blame her brother's unexpected schedule change, along with the fact that Harrison had yet to officially inform Lexy about it. The last-minute switch gave Tanner reason to throw up his hands, tell her this wasn't his fault and the auction came first.

But he'd seen the nervous peeks at her phone, the hurt in her eyes growing every minute there was no ring. No way he'd throw logs on the fire. Whatever had strained her relationship with her brother, Tanner wouldn't heap on more pain. It would kill him to lose Doug's trust and respect, and he felt confident the reverse was true, as well. Even with their being opposites, the bond was strong.

Ironically, whether she wanted it or not, Lexy had Tanner's sympathy. She sure had his attention, too. He brought the T-shirt up over her head, tossed it and unfastened her bra. She let it slide off then tugged his T-shirt free of his jeans. They seemed to realize at the same time there was a faster way to get naked. Boots, shoes and socks first, then they were each stripping off their own jeans.

"Did you bring in the condoms?" she asked, eyes widening.

"Are you kidding? I'd sooner forget my Stetson."

She laughed, familiar with how he felt about that poor, worn hat. It was kind of odd how many little things she knew about him in such a short period of time. Things that had taken Doreen months to get. Or maybe she'd never made the connections Lexy had.

He stopped her from pulling down her panties. He wanted that pleasure to be his. Starting with a kiss on her lips, he slid down to roll his tongue over her beaded nipple. With a soft moan, she arched into his mouth and clutched at his hair. He would've lingered if he hadn't wanted those panties off so badly.

Pressing his lips to the silky skin under her ribs, he slid his palm up the back of her thighs and cupped her bottom. When he withdrew, she protested with a frustrated groan and a tug of his hair. Smiling, he reached behind and started the tub water before turning back to yank down her panties.

She let out a small yelp of surprise, then held on to his shoulder and slipped one foot free. "You sneaky little— Oh."

He'd spread her freed leg wide and kissed between her thighs. She was warm and moist and smelled so good that he could've spent an hour right there. Lexy quivered and pushed him away.

"First, we get rid of these," she said, and worked her splayed hands under the waistband of his boxers.

She molded her palms to his hips, her fingers lightly digging into his ass, before she moved to grip his hard cock.

He sucked in a shuddering breath. "Easy or we won't make it into the tub."

"We will eventually." She stroked upward, thumbing the crown.

The knock on the door made them both groan. "The wine," they said in unison.

She picked up his jeans and handed them to him. "You can do the honors since it was your great idea."

"Don't you fret." He leaned in for a kiss. "We have all night." Except they didn't. How the hell could he have forgotten? "After you bring me luck at poker." Coward that he was, he ducked his head to pull up his jeans.

"Poker? Is that a joke?"

"There's a high-stakes game tonight," he said, glancing up. "If I'm lucky, a big win could take care of that cash-flow problem."

"And if you're not?"

"Hell, I'm already screwed."

She studied his face, probably looking for a reason not to haul off and smack him. Whatever she saw there must've satisfied her, because she slowly nodded, and turned to test the water filling the tub.

Or maybe it had nothing to do with being satisfied, and everything to do with being resigned.

Maybe she'd just decided to cut her losses.

15

THE WESTERN-THEMED RESTAURANT with its rustic tables and chairs, red-gingham curtains and matching vinyl table-cloths looked as though it could be a family place. Though Lexy couldn't imagine any parents in their right minds bringing kids here. The bar in the back needed more than swinging doors to keep the raucous laughter and ripe language contained.

But then it was after ten, and it appeared they'd stopped serving food already. The older woman standing at the register had looked up when they entered, smiled and went back to counting money as they passed her to go through the swinging doors.

Their entry into the bar met with momentary silence. The couple throwing darts gave them a fleeting look before returning to their game. The men crowding the bar were drinking beer, eating peanuts from a large bowl and tossing shells on the wooden floor. A cowboy sitting at the end apparently recognized Tanner and nodded, the surprise on his face quite clear.

The bearded bartender looked out of place, more like a biker with his long, graying hair pulled back in a ponytail. He squinted at Tanner then motioned with his eyes at a door marked Private.

Even though Tanner had explained the place was a favorite watering hole for rodeo riders, and that the owner hosted a monthly high-stakes game, everything felt surreal. As if they'd slipped through a portal back in time. She imagined a speakeasy may have looked like this. It didn't help that Tanner's plan was completely crazy and went against everything she thought she knew about him.

"What? No password or secret handshake?" she whispered, trying to lighten the mood, hers mostly.

Smiling thinly, he squeezed her hand, the one he'd held for the entire three-block walk. "You sure you're okay with being here? I can still take you back to the hotel."

"No, I want to watch." What she really wanted was for them to both be in the room with a Do-Not-Disturb sign hanging from their door. "Anyway, I'm supposed to be your amulet."

She wondered if her confusion and a bad case of nerves could somehow cancel out any luck she might bring him. Perhaps the thought had occurred to him, too. He released her hand the second they entered the well-lit room.

Four older men playing cards at the table stopped briefly to check out the newcomers. So did the pair standing in the corner talking. Both of them acknowledged Tanner as if they knew him. At the opposite side of the room, a tall, slim, blonde woman mixing drinks gave him a big smile.

"Hey, cowboy, long time no see." She set down a bottle of whiskey, wiped her hands on a towel and came around the portable bar to throw her arms around him. "I was shocked to hear you were coming." She kissed his cheek, leaving behind a smear of pink lipstick.

Well, not really his cheek, more like the side of his mouth. Lexy was fairly certain the woman had only missed his lips because Tanner turned his face at the last second.

"How you doing, Sherry?" He yanked his hat off. "Besides getting prettier while the rest of us are just getting older."

She laughed and swatted his arm. "My kids would tell you I'm getting crankier. But they're teenagers, so what do they know? Other than *everything.*" Sherry smiled at Lexy. "Will you be joining the fellas tonight?"

"She's with me," Tanner said, and introduced them.

He stayed close, but didn't take her hand again. Or touch her or introduce her to any of the men. Anyone watching would think they were casual friends, which was the truth. If she thought otherwise she'd be foolish. Once they arrived in Houston and she handed him over, she'd return to Oklahoma City, and Tanner would be off doing…she had no idea what he would do next.

The thought didn't sit well. Though frankly, she doubted she knew him at all. None of what he was doing made sense. Until a few hours ago, he'd seemed like the most steady, stable, secure man she'd ever met.

But in the short time since they'd arrived, he'd had money wired to him, drawn a sizeable cash advance against his only credit card, arranged for a marker with whoever was in charge of the game and was ready to pretty much "bet the farm." All this, when a few days ago, he'd claimed he never had and never would play high-stakes poker. Yes, of course she knew he needed fast cash, but that he was willing to lose everything on the *chance* he could win didn't fall in sync with his character.

Sherry left to finish making drinks, but before Lexy could say anything to Tanner, a short, wiry man about his age approached them. He politely nodded to her when Tanner introduced them, then Colby said in a low voice, "I'm already wiped out for the night. Can you believe it?"

Tanner frowned. "How long you been playing?"

"Me? A couple hours at best." He removed his hat and scratched his head. "J.D. cleaned my clock. The bastard's been hot for six days straight. Unreal. I've never seen anything like it."

They were both staring at the dark-haired cowboy with the graying temples, leaning back in his chair and focusing on the cards fanned out in his hand. His weathered face made his age indiscernible, but Lexy would guess he was around sixty.

"Why are you even here?" Colby's eyes narrowed on Tanner. "You never play for this kind of scratch, and tell you what…now ain't the time to start." He darted a look at the table, then turned his head and spoke close to Tanner's ear. "Second day in he won a Caddy off some poor slob who'd run out of money and markers."

"I heard," Tanner said, his gaze trained on J.D.

"Hey…" With a bewildered expression, Colby studied Tanner. "You've never gone up against him, have you?"

"Nope. Any idea how much he's up?"

"Sherry thinks it's close to eighty grand. And that's after buying everyone drinks and chow all week. Rocky might as well put a revolving door out front. Guys have been coming outta the woodwork hoping to break his streak. Everyone's been betting big."

"How big?"

"Don't be stupid, Tanner."

Lexy wanted to give Colby a hug for saying what she couldn't. Not that Tanner was paying any attention. He seemed transfixed by what was happening at the table. She bumped him slightly with her shoulder, hoping to snap him out of his trance. He didn't budge. Just kept studying the older man in the brown plaid shirt.

Colby glanced at her as if Tanner's being here was somehow her fault. "Remember Bob Samuels two years ago?" he said to Tanner. "He ran hot for ten days, won over a hundred grand and ended up going home flat broke. So did a lot of other guys."

She couldn't stand it another minute and touched his arm. "Tanner? Please think about this." She spoke quietly so that no one heard except for Colby.

At least Tanner broke eye contact with the game to look at her. "I don't want to be here, believe me," he said, and brushed a strand of hair off her cheek.

Colby cleared his throat. "I'm outta here," he said. "Good luck. Better yet, listen to the lady and get."

Tanner watched Colby claim his hat from a wall peg behind Sherry, then nodded to him as he left.

When he brought his gaze back to her, Lexy lifted a hand to his face. "Lipstick," she said, rubbing the pink smear off with her thumb.

He caught her fisted hand. "Relax," he said, forcing her fingers open. "I know what I'm doing." He kissed her palm, his eyes locked with hers.

She wasn't so sure he did. People had seemed shocked to see Tanner, so she hadn't been too far off the mark about him. But what was going on with his family that would make him desperate enough to step out of character?

"Your hand's cold." He kissed the back this time, and then sandwiched it between his warm, calloused palms. He seemed calm and steady, no sign of nerves, but of course that wasn't so surprising. His job was riding powerful broncs determined to buck him to high heaven.

She swallowed, but it didn't help the lump in her throat. "He's watching us." Her gaze had flickered away for a second. "The man in the plaid shirt. J.D.?"

"I'm sure he is."

Noise erupted from the players. Two of them cussed viciously. J.D. grinned and started raking in piles of different-colored chips from the center of the table.

The man in the black T-shirt just shook his head and threw down his cards. "That's it for me." He scraped his chair back from the table, stood and rubbed his bloodshot eyes. "Your goddamn luck is gonna run out sooner or later, J.D."

A husky, balding man, his arms folded over his paunch, leaned sideways to whisper something to Sherry. She nodded, pulled a notebook from behind the bar and held it out to him.

"Hey, Tanner, we need to get you squared away," the man said. "The guys are taking ten while we wait for a fifth player. Joe should be here any minute."

"Be right there." Tanner continued to rub her hand. "Don't look so worried. Everything's gonna be fine, Lexy. I promise."

"Don't." She looked into his eyes, not caring if her disappointment showed. "You can't make that promise because there's no guarantee you'll win."

"Technically, you're right. But this isn't as crazy as it seems. Consider this a calculated risk."

She stared helplessly at him. "I don't understand any of it, but it's your business."

He searched her face for a moment, looking as if he wanted to tell her something more. But all he said was, "You can still wait at the hotel."

"No, I'll be too nervous."

He gave her a faint smile. "How about a kiss for luck?" Without waiting for an answer, he lowered his head and brushed a soft kiss across her lips.

She had a feeling everyone was watching them, and she didn't care. She wound her arms around him and hugged him close. "I do wish you luck," she whispered. "But I hope you understand gambling can never be considered a calculated risk."

"You're right," he said, moving back. "My bet is on J.D. I know him, and I know I can beat him." Tanner glanced at J.D. just as he looked up.

Staring into the older man's face, Lexy finally saw the resemblance.

J.D. was his father.

TWO HOURS LATER, Tanner was up by three thousand dollars. On a normal poker night, he'd be as pleased as a flea in a doghouse. In fact, he'd have cashed out by now. But there was nothing ordinary about this game, and with Lexy anxiously watching, he had to really narrow his focus so he wouldn't feel like such a chump.

He knew she disapproved, and he didn't blame her. This wasn't one of his finer moments. He'd sworn years ago he'd never sit across a poker table from his father. It wouldn't be a fair match. J.D.'s guilt would trip him up. And though Tanner wasn't proud of it, that's exactly what he was counting on.

The player who'd shown up late, Joe Baker, was a saddle bronc rider Tanner knew fairly well. The other two men sitting at the table had quit rodeoing shortly after he'd started competing professionally. While he was familiar with their reputations as World Champion Team Ropers, he didn't personally know Chet and Larry. Sherry had warned him that both men now owned large cattle operations in Wyoming, were good players and had deep pockets.

Maybe Tanner should've been more concerned about them. But he already knew that a high-stakes game like this attracted two types of players…skilled competitors or men with more money than sense. Tanner fell somewhere in between. Except he normally had better sense. And then there was J.D., who'd lucked into a seat at the "big boys" table.

Tanner sat across from him. They'd made eye contact a few times before the game started, even nodded to each other, but they hadn't exchanged words. His father was curious, though, that much Tanner knew, and if that curiosity threw J.D. off his game some, Tanner hoped it was in his favor.

It was Joe's turn. He studied his cards with undisguised frustration. No guessing what he was about to do. He shook his head, sighed in disgust and threw his cards facedown. Sure wasn't his night. Folding two out of three times made a stack of chips dwindle fast.

Larry muttered a mild curse and folded.

Rocky owned the restaurant and bar, and was also the dealer. He looked to Chet and waited. Chet kept his eyes on his cards and his mouth in a tight, unreadable line. His fingers hovered over his stacks of black chips. "I'll raise," he said finally, and threw in three hundred-dollar chips.

"Call," Tanner said, without looking at his cards again. But he did keep his attention on J.D., who avoided his gaze. If Tanner was reading his father correctly, he'd fold.

"J.D.?" Rocky prompted.

He hesitated, grunted and discarded his hand.

It was between Tanner and Chet. The man didn't have a single tell that Tanner could identify. Chet narrowed his dark eyes on the sizeable pot, then threw down his cards.

Turned out to be a big win for Tanner. But he made the mistake of glancing at Lexy while he raked in his chips. Saw the way she nervously bit at her lower lip. Man, he really wished he'd left her at the hotel. It took more effort than he'd imagined to shut her out of his mind. Twice he'd caught himself daydreaming about taking her back to the room and making love again on that big king bed.

"Sorry, boys, but I gotta take a piss again," Joe said. "It's all that damn coffee I drank trying to stay awake on the road." He rose, shaking his head at the pitifully small stack of chips he had left on the table. "Don't know how much longer I'm gonna last."

Rocky stopped shuffling and laid down the deck of cards. "How about we take ten?"

Chet checked his watch as he got to his feet. "Let's make it five."

"Fine." Larry stretched his neck to the side.

Rocky looked to J.D. and Tanner, and they both agreed. Wanting to avoid getting stuck alone with his father, Tanner got up and went to Lexy.

"Are you done?" she asked, leaving the chair Sherry had brought in for her, and cradling a tumbler in her hands.

"Sorry." He watched the momentary excitement drain from her face. "It's just a break. What are you drinking?"

"I'm not sure. Bourbon, maybe?" With a shrug, she offered him the amber liquid. "Sherry thought I could use it."

Tanner smiled. "No, thanks. I don't drink when I play."

"Right. Makes sense." Lexy sighed and took a small sip.

He gave her a brief kiss. "Yep, bourbon."

She let out a laugh. "It's my second one and I still feel like bouncing off the walls."

"Go back to the hotel, sweetheart." He ran a hand up her arm and felt her shiver. "I shouldn't have brought you."

"It was my choice," she said stiffly, then widened her eyes. "Do I make you nervous? Am I distracting you?"

"You're fine." It was the high stakes testing his backbone. He glanced toward the table. J.D. hadn't moved and openly watched them.

"Is it always this quiet and serious?"

"Well, like I said, I've never played for this kind of money. I really do stick to friendly games. I might lose a hundred bucks but everyone can still laugh and joke."

"It looks as if you're ahead. May I ask how much, or will that jinx you?" Those earnest blue eyes of hers sure could get to him.

He touched her cheek. "You know I'm doing this only because my back's against the wall." His chest tightened when she said nothing, only blinked, the movement slow and thoughtful. "Lexy, tell me you understand."

"I trust you." She pushed up on tiptoes and kissed his mouth.

"Come on, lover boy," Rocky called out. "Get back here."

Joe, Chet and Larry had already returned to the table. Their punchy laughter echoed their tired, red-rimmed eyes. They all needed to find bunks more than they needed to play another round. That boded well for Tanner. He felt rested. J.D. had quietly smiled and kept his gaze on the deck Rocky was shuffling.

An hour later, with only about a hundred bucks left in chips, Joe called it quits. He made a joke about having enough money for gas to get to the Cheyenne rodeo, then left the chips for Sherry as a tip. Rocky would get his cut of the winnings for hosting the game. Nobody had to worry about Joe. He'd collected over two-hundred grand in prize money last year.

Half an hour after that, Larry shocked everyone by announcing he was done. He was up by eighty-two hundred but he'd been playing for twelve hours and claimed he couldn't see straight anymore. Rocky suggested they take another break and no one objected.

Chet and Rocky got up so fast, Tanner didn't have time to escape the dreaded moment of being left alone with J.D.

"How's Doug?" J.D. asked.

"Fine. Great."

"He still living in Dallas?"

Tanner nodded and looked over at Lexy. She stared back, gripping her glass with two hands and taking small sips of her drink. No telling how many she'd had by now. He hoped she didn't get sick.

"That's a real pretty girl you've got there, son."

Tanner gritted his teeth. The man had no goddamn right to call him son. Hell, he was probably trying to rile him. Tanner mentally shook it off. Shame on him if he let J.D. get to him.

"How about your grandparents? How are they doing?"

"Not so good."

"Are they sick?" J.D. actually sounded concerned.

Tanner looked at him, totally unprepared for the sincerity in his hazel eyes. "No. I don't think so. Look, I gotta go—"

"What about you, Will?" his father asked. "I saw you ride in Billings. Everybody knew they opened the chute before you gave the nod. You should've gotten a reride."

"Wouldn't have mattered. I got hung up on the gate and hurt the arm I broke three months before."

"What's that, three times now you've busted that arm?" J.D. chuckled. "You always were a tough kid."

Tanner almost pointed out that J.D. hadn't been there for his childhood, so how the hell did he know. But it would be useless. So was paying any heed to the unexpected pride in the old man's voice. All that shit was probably meant to throw Tanner off his game, anyway. He pushed away from the table.

"Will?"

He stood, but paused, waiting for whatever J.D. had to say. As long as it was quick.

"You don't play high-stakes poker. Why are you here, son?"

Tanner thought for a moment. He really wanted to tell him to shut the hell up. But his own guilt forced his silence. Ironic, really, since J.D.'s guilt was the reason Tanner had never played poker with him. Somehow it hadn't seemed fair since he had an advantage. Tanner still remembered the remorse and shame he'd seen in the old man's eyes the day of his mom's funeral.

She shouldn't have been fighting in some foreign country. She should've been home raising her two boys. But J.D. had left her with little money and few options. And since the day they put her in the ground, he hadn't been able to face Tanner without the truth rearing up like a pissed-off bronc, his front hooves pawing the sky.

That's why Tanner had been sure he could beat him. And he'd been one hundred percent right. Every time J.D. had a hand he thought would beat Tanner, a tiny flicker of guilt flashed in his eyes.

He didn't answer J.D., just shook his head and walked over to Lexy. "Did you hear?" he asked her. "Larry dropped out."

"That doesn't mean the game's over, though."

"No, but Chet is getting bleary-eyed. He ran hot for a while, but he's only doing so-so now. I suspect he'll call it a night soon." He looked into her uncertain eyes and took the glass from her hands. "You getting a little drunk?"

"Are you kidding? I'm too wired."

He took a sip of the bourbon. Just a small one. Soon it would be only him and his old man sitting at that table. He put the tumbler back in her hands, hating the worried expression that dimmed her beautiful eyes.

"You need another good-luck kiss?" she asked, moving closer and tilting her head back.

"It's worked so far."

She smiled up at him. "Well, come on, lover boy."

Damn, he hoped she'd still be smiling after he told her they weren't going straight to Houston tomorrow.

16

LEXY REALLY WISHED she'd cooled it on the bourbon. She wasn't drunk but her jittery stomach strongly objected to the alcohol. Abandoning the chair, she moved closer to the table so she could see what was happening. Although Chet had cashed in his chips thirty minutes ago, he'd stuck around to watch the game. His buddy Larry had returned, not to play, but as a spectator, his clothes reeking of cigarette smoke. Another younger man with a distinct limp had appeared out of nowhere and joined them. Then Sherry had left the bar to stand beside Chet and completely block Lexy's view.

As little as she knew about poker, it seemed clear the game was building to a head. New rules pertinent to the game, now that it was down to two players, had been explained and acknowledged. A staggering number of chips were stacked in front of both Tanner and his father. Not all the same color, though, so Lexy couldn't determine who was ahead money-wise. But that's what it would come down to. It was always about money. Those who had it, and those who didn't. If not for her own struggles the past few years, she never would've had the thought.

Tanner leaned back and drank deeply from the bottle of water Sherry had given him. Rocky dealt out the cards.

J.D. hunched forward, but he didn't seem nervous. He was simply shifting positions. They were each given two cards facedown, and then Rocky dealt three cards faceup in the middle of the table. Tanner set the water aside, dragged his palm down the leg of his jeans and picked up his cards, looked at them, his expression completely blank.

J.D. was already studying his cards with an impassive face much like his son's. When the betting started Lexy could barely breathe. The astounding amounts being traded back and forth seemed crazy, and yet there'd been a time when she thought nothing of spending ten thousand dollars on a purse.

Still, she couldn't just stand there. She paced instead, wishing the room were bigger. With Chet and Larry standing shoulder to shoulder and Sherry beside them, Lexy didn't worry about being a distraction. No one could see her, even if they were paying attention, which they weren't. She pressed a hand to her roiling stomach, knowing that in a matter of minutes, Tanner would have the money he needed or he'd be flat broke.

God, how much she wished she could've helped him. It wasn't as though she were a pauper. She had money sitting in her damn trust fund accruing interest. Her stubborn father was the problem. Squeezing her eyes shut, she massaged her left temple until the sudden throbbing dulled. That wasn't true. Her stupid pride had always been just as formidable a stumbling block.

She breathed in deeply, as clearheaded as she'd ever felt. If Tanner lost, she had only one option. She'd have to call her father. Let him think he'd finally crushed her spirit, bent her will to his if she had to. Pride would never wipe the bitter taste of letting Tanner down.

The onlookers let out a collective gasp. Lexy shut down all thoughts but those of Tanner. She tried to squeeze in between him and Chet, but the man was as broad as a linebacker. He wasn't moving. She doubted he noticed she was even there, and she settled for standing just behind Tanner's left shoulder.

"Tell you what, son." J.D. laid his cards facedown, folded his hands and looked Tanner in the eyes. "What do you say we end this here? Right now. We can both walk away with a nice chunk of change."

Lexy saw that most of J.D.'s chips were no longer in front of him but in the middle of the table. So that's why everyone had been so shocked. She hoped like hell Tanner would accept his father's offer.

"What's wrong, J.D.?" he said. "You losing your nerve?"

A slight frown drew the older man's brows together. "Is that what you really think?"

Tanner held his cards at an angle only he could see. "What I thought was that we were here to play poker."

Rocky rubbed the bald spot on his head and sighed like a man who'd been awake too long and was running out of patience. "You fellas better make up your minds. Play now, talk later, or we call it a night."

"We're playing," Tanner said in a terse voice, his gaze never wavering from his father. "I'll call," he said, shoving his pile of chips forward. "And I'll raise you."

"I don't believe you will," J.D. said quietly.

"I just said so, didn't I?"

"You ain't got enough." His father's emotionless gaze lowered to Tanner's chips before slowly returning to his face.

"Well, hell, I believe he's right, Tanner." Rocky's keen black eyes seemed to do a quick counting. "Sherry, help him restack and count."

Tanner's bravado faltered. He stared down at what had to be over fifty thousand in chips. "Give me another marker, Rocky." His stricken expression tore at Lexy's heart. "You know I'm good for it."

"Yep, I do." Rocky shook his head, his face full of regret. "But I can't. You know the rules."

"Come on, Will. Let it go." J.D. pushed back his chair. "We're done. Take your money."

"Wait." He watched Sherry restack and group chips with amazing dexterity. "You can't walk off. We're still in play while she's counting."

J.D. looked at Rocky, who nodded confirmation.

"Tanner?" Lexy touched his arm. He didn't even look at her.

"Tell you what," he said, locking gazes with his father. "I'll throw in a buckle."

Lexy had a heart-stopping feeling she knew what he meant. The sudden silence shrouding the room told her she was right. He wanted to put up his world champion gold buckle. In professional rodeo, relatively few men ever realized their dream of that coveted prize.

Larry and Chet were shaking their heads. "Jesus, Tanner, don't be stupid," Chet said. "Walk away now. There's no shame in it. You lose that buckle, you'll hate yourself for the rest of your life."

Chet knew what he was talking about. According to Sherry, he'd earned three gold buckles. Even she had stopped counting and stared at Tanner as if he were out of his mind.

He ignored everyone. "Come on, J.D., isn't that what you've always wanted? There was a time when you would've sold your soul for a gold buckle. As a matter of fact—" Tanner blinked and cut himself short.

Before he crossed a line he'd never be able to uncross.

He didn't say, but everyone knew it. Lexy could only imagine what hurtful thing had nearly tripped off the tip of his tongue. His father had failed him and his brother, their mother. She had no idea who knew their history, but no one could miss the anguish simmering between the two men.

Tanner slumped back and sighed. The fight had left him. "Do it, Dad," he said quietly. "For me."

"Look, son," J.D. began, and Tanner squeezed his eyes shut.

"Wait." Lexy practically shoved Chet out of her way. She pulled off her Rolex. "Here. Take this." She addressed J.D., pleading with her eyes. "It's solid gold, real diamonds, worth about forty thousand."

"No." Tanner tried to pull back her hand. "No, Alexis. I won't let you." He reached for the watch but she evaded him and laid it on the mound of chips. "It was your grandmother's," he murmured tightly.

"It's just a watch, Tanner," she said. "I'm not letting you give up your buckle. It's not like you can get another one." She glanced at J.D., and he gave her a small nod.

"No."

"Dammit, Tanner, shut up. Just shut up." She trapped his face between her hands and kissed him hard, hard enough that his head went back with the force. He caught one of her wrists but she kept kissing him, using her tongue and teeth and anything she thought would keep him distracted until the game had to continue.

Finally, with gentle force, he pushed her back. "Jesus, Lexy, what the hell?"

With a lift of her chin, she sniffed and smoothed her hair. "That's not how you usually react."

Chet grinned.

Sherry laughed.

"Okay." Rocky, who'd earlier looked as if he'd been dying to say something, quickly dealt a card. "The game's in play."

"Bullshit." Tanner's dazed expression and uneven breathing filled her with satisfaction.

"You heard the dealer," J.D. said gruffly. "Not our fault you can't control your woman."

Lexy's mouth dropped open. But he'd agreed to take her watch so she held her tongue. Then she saw the corner of his mouth twitch with humor. Well, why not? He would probably be leaving with her Rolex. She didn't care. Tanner was more important.

Too bad he looked miserable. For a moment she feared she'd completely ruined everything between them. She leaned close to say something reassuring…and froze.

The words going off like fireworks in her head literally made her knees weak.

She'd almost admitted she loved him. The truth stole her breath. She backed up a step. It wasn't possible to fall in love that quickly. Any fool knew that much.

But then she'd never been in love. Puppy love, yes. In lust, yes. Infatuation, probably. But not real love. Not the crazy, stupid feeling that made your head fuzzy enough to give away your gold watch. How many times had she considered pawning the Rolex to pay rent, buy food and gas, get the credit card companies off her back? She'd tried that one time, and hastily reclaimed it. At the end of the day, she'd decided she'd rather live in her car than give up her grandmother's cherished gift.

But she knew Tanner needed to keep his buckle, and she hadn't thought twice. Letting the impulsiveness of her actions sink in, she still had no regret. Given the chance, she'd do it all over again. Was that love?

The sudden noise startled her. Sherry had let out a squeal. Chet's abrupt laugh bellowed off the walls.

Stunned, Lexy realized she'd missed the last play of the game. She couldn't see Tanner's face, so she risked a glance at J.D. Her heart lurched. He didn't look like a man who'd just lost a ton of money. But then, he didn't seem happy, either. Which confused her all the more.

Chet clapped Tanner on the back then gave her a huge hug that had her gasping for air. Only then did it sink in that Tanner had won. The final card hadn't needed to be dealt because J.D. had folded.

Tanner leaned back in his chair and pushed his hands through his hair. He turned to look at her, his expression suspended somewhere between shock and relief.

She smiled, then got out of the way when Sherry threw her arms around him and nearly lifted him out of the chair. Rocky stood, put a hand on J.D.'s shoulder and said something only he could hear. In spite of everything, Lexy felt bad for the man. Not so much about losing the money, but because everyone seemed overwhelmingly glad for Tanner.

To his credit, J.D. simply shrugged, his mouth curved in a faint smile as he sat there watching everyone else celebrate. Rocky moved off to congratulate Tanner, and J.D. glanced at her. She hadn't meant to look directly into his dark, hazel eyes. She expected resentment, but saw only pain.

He averted his gaze, leaned over the table and picked up her watch from the pile of chips. Very carefully he used the hem of his plaid shirt to polish smudges off the crystal, then held out the Rolex to her.

She took the few steps to reach him, her heart still pounding out of control. "Thank you," she said, accepting the watch, touched by his thoughtful gesture.

Nodding, he pushed away from the table. "Will's a good man," he murmured quietly. "No thanks to me." He rose abruptly, giving her the impression he wanted to avoid coming off as sentimental. "Seems you two really have something. Don't take it for granted."

He met her eyes again, and gave her a small nod as he pushed his chair to the table. Lexy moved back to give him room to exit. Apprehension flickered across his face and he turned back with a worried frown. Calmly, he picked up the cards he'd left facedown and slipped them into the remaining deck.

Lexy wasn't trying, but she saw the aces before they disappeared. Little as she knew about poker, she understood that Tanner's father had folded on a winning hand.

BEHIND HIS SUNGLASSES, Tanner squinted at the highway sign for Amarillo and stifled a yawn. Lexy unscrewed the thermos of coffee and passed it to him. He swore the woman had some sort of radar.

"For the record," she said, "I still think we should stop at a motel so you can get more sleep. I feel better that we're already in Texas. Don't you?"

He wouldn't feel better until he'd told her the whole truth, made it to the auction, bought his grandparents' ranch and got to Houston in time for the silly photo shoot. Then, and only then, would he be able to relax. This morning he'd sworn to himself she'd know everything before they left the hotel. But he kept thinking about what she'd done last night. For him. He still had trouble believing it. Would she feel he'd deserved her sacrifice once she knew how he'd misled her?

When he'd initially learned of the auction, he could justify his decision to not tell her everything. Easy, since he'd been in the dark himself. He'd also been protecting her from unnecessary worry. He'd known they'd get to Houston in time.

But then things had changed quickly between them. It seemed that in the space of a day Lexy had become important to him. She wasn't a good-time gal looking to pass a few pleasant nights with a rodeo champion. They'd told each other stuff, they'd gotten up-close and personal about their pasts and feelings.

He breathed in deeply. And yet he hadn't been able to admit what was troubling him the most. He'd failed Pop and Nana. A truly *good* grandson would have known the ranch was in trouble. That's what hurt the most. He'd tried his best, but obviously his grandparents hadn't believed they could count on him.

Had he been too busy worrying about taking his last ride as a winner to notice they'd been scraping by? He'd won two world championships. Thousands of guys never came close to that honor, couldn't even make it on the pro tour. He'd been damn lucky. There was no shame in stepping aside for the new crop of cowboys who wanted to fulfill their childhood dreams. Just as he had done. That was the way of things. But even that wasn't the issue.

Man, he couldn't be that guy who chose the rodeo and his ego over his family. That was his father. Not him. And yet that hollow feeling in his gut wouldn't let him off the hook. If he was the man he thought he was, Pop and Nana wouldn't be in this predicament. They would've reached out to him.

The bitter truth was hard enough to swallow. Now he had to face the sorry fact that he was also a friggin' coward. He'd purposely duped Lexy, and she didn't deserve that. He should've laid out the problem as soon as he knew what was what. If she decided he was a lousy grandson and a bastard for lying, so be it.

And now he wasn't sure how to clean up his mess without causing more damage.

After taking a gulp of coffee, he gave her back the thermos. She smiled, and for a moment he convinced himself that everything would work out fine. As long as he was successful at the auction, and then got them to Houston in time, that's all that mattered. He rubbed her arm, enjoying the silky feel of her warm skin. His good luck had run beyond poker and winning championships. How was it possible he'd found this amazing woman?

"Tanner, I'm serious. You had only four hours' sleep last night."

"So did you."

"But I'm not driving. Although maybe I should. You've had quite the heavy foot today."

"We'll stop in an hour and see how we feel." He eased off the accelerator and returned his hand to the wheel. "I promise."

It had been more like three hours' sleep, but she didn't need to know that. Adrenaline had kept him revved long after the game had ended, long after she'd dozed off in his arms. He still couldn't believe she'd been willing to give up her watch for him. With all her struggles, she could've sold it, made her life easier for a while. She'd refused to give in. Yet she hadn't hesitated to jump in when he was in need.

The thought slapped him with another coat of shame. When she'd first offered the Rolex he'd felt humbled. But part of her argument reminded him he didn't have a chance at winning another gold buckle. He knew what she'd meant, but it had upset him at first. And even if she had been trying to tell him he was washed up, it was the truth. She wasn't the coward, he was.

"I'm glad you left some money for J.D.," Lexy said out of the blue.

Tanner sighed. "I hope he took it."

"Me, too," she murmured, almost to herself, then glanced at her phone.

Again, he had the feeling she was keeping something from him, too. He'd sensed it yesterday and earlier this morning. But he'd chalked it up to his own guilty conscience. Or maybe her shifting mood had to do with her brother. The jerk still hadn't told her about moving up the photo shoot. Or returned her call.

"Of course it depends on how the bidding goes tomorrow. But anything I don't need I'm returning to J.D., and then—" From his peripheral vision, he saw her turn sharply to him. "What? I didn't want to play against him. I was desperate. I'll still give him back most of the money, even though, technically, I won it fair and square. I'm not a total bastard."

She was still staring at him. "You said tomorrow."

His mouth went bone dry at his mistake. "Tomorrow what?"

"The auction. Don't you mean in three days?"

Had he actually said that? He couldn't even remember what lie he'd told. Only that the deception had swelled in his throat and now he was having trouble swallowing. He saw a sign for a travel stop five miles ahead. "I'm gonna pull off at the next exit and we'll talk."

"So the auction *is* tomorrow." Her voice drooped with disappointment. "Why didn't you tell me?"

"Can we please wait for me to park so I can explain?"

"Why not?" She turned to stare out her window. "You've waited this long."

"Lexy, don't."

"Don't what?" She looked back at him, her brows raised, one shoulder lifting in casual indifference. "Be disappointed? Be angry? Feel like an idiot?" Her eyes closed briefly. When she opened them again, her expression was so bleak, it hurt to look at her. "So many things make sense now. You never planned to go to Houston, did you?"

"That's not true. I told you I'd go and I meant it. I didn't know this thing would happen with my grandparents." Someone behind him honked. He looked at the speedometer and winced. He must've braked and disengaged cruise control because he was driving like an old lady. He pressed the gas and brought them up to the speed limit. "The second the auction is over, we'll drive to Houston. We're going to make it on time. I give you my word."

Her sigh of disgust spelled out just how little his word meant to her. Much as he deserved her disappointment, it still hurt. Man, he hoped she was just overtired, that they could talk this out. He was willing to own the mistake, but would that be enough?

"Lexy, there's something else about the auction I didn't tell you."

"Gee, what a surprise." She slipped on her sunglasses before turning back to him. "Look, you're doing this for your grandparents. You had to make a hard choice. I get it. I do. I even admire your loyalty. What I don't understand is why you couldn't be honest with me. Instead, you manipulated me…just like—" Her voice broke and she faced the window again.

Like who? Her father? That wasn't fair. "I never manipulated you. I just wasn't quick to tell you the whole story—" He paused to exit the expressway, the confession sticking in his throat. "It's their ranch. The one I'll be bidding on. They lost it to back taxes." He kept his eyes on the road, hoping to avoid more of her disappointment. "So yeah, admiring my loyalty to family? Scratch that off the list. I had no clue they were in trouble. I'm a damn lousy grandson. What can I say?"

"Lousy… What, because they didn't come to you for money?"

He shrugged, suddenly bone weary.

"Perhaps they didn't ask for your help because you've already done so much for Doug, and I'm guessing for them, as well?"

"So? We're talking about their ranch, not a broken generator. Yet they didn't feel they could discuss it with me?"

"Sounds familiar. Avoidance must run in your family."

Tanner clenched his jaw. His playing loose with the truth wasn't the same thing. He was always going to tell her, it had been a matter of timing. And his intention to make it to Houston had never wavered. They would still be there for the photo shoot. That had to count for something.

"You don't understand why I'm upset, do you?" Lexy

asked the second he parked the truck outside a convenience store. She waited until he looked at her, though both of them were hiding behind their sunglasses. "From the moment I rejected Harvard, I had to fight for my individuality and freedom and not allow my father to dictate my life. I struggled financially, emotionally and many times I came close to crumbling because I wasn't prepared to give up the privileged life I'd taken for granted.

"But I didn't give in, and it about killed me to go to my father for a job. I told myself it wasn't groveling because it's a family business. It didn't matter. It felt like begging, and I hated every second sitting in that office, suffering his condescension while he mapped out this ridiculous plan to humble me." She sucked in a shaky breath. "Now you tell me…after all that, do you really think I need you deciding what's good for me? You should've trusted me with the truth and not fooled yourself that you were saving me worry." She paused, and lowered her chin. "I deserved to be given a choice about Houston. I still would've done anything to help you."

He studied her ashen face. "Would you have?" he asked, and her brows rose above the dark lenses. "I mean, it's easy to play Monday morning quarterback. And I don't doubt you'd like to think you would've made that choice. You and I both know me showing up at the photo shoot is a joke, yet you've gone to extraordinary lengths to get me there. So maybe we're both fooling ourselves."

Her lips parted and color returned to her cheeks. She didn't speak, just stared at him from behind the dark lenses.

He sighed, trying to figure out if he should regret digging a deeper hole. Hell, she wanted the truth. "I wish I could undo the past few days. I can't, but I can try to make things right with us." He rubbed the back of his neck. "Lexy, I get it. I was wrong and you have every reason not to trust me. I understand."

She stayed silent, but what did it matter? He'd known this thing between them would end sooner or later. He slept in a trailer. She liked suites. His carefree lifestyle suited him.

He didn't have to answer to anyone and he had a lot of fish to catch in the near future. Screw it. Why complicate his life now?

"I don't think you do," she said softly. "I don't think you understand at all."

"Sure I do." He restarted the engine. "What I did was kinda like you throwing your watch in the pot. Pretty big decision you made for me. No question your intentions were good. But if I'd lost that hand, I would've felt like shit for a hell of a long time."

17

ABOUT A MILE down the gravel road Tanner turned left into his grandparents' narrow driveway. Lexy couldn't see the house yet, but she knew it was a small brick ranch with three bedrooms on forty acres because Tanner had told her that when the tense, silent ride had gotten to them. Three hours seemed like a lifetime when two people didn't have much to say to one another.

The town was so small it hadn't taken long for him to track down his grandparents. They'd been staying at a friend's house while they packed up the last of their belongings at the ranch. Tanner knew they were there now, finishing up. He was in a terrible mood, and not just because of his earlier disagreement with Lexy. He'd learned that Archie, the neighbor who'd called him, had passed on wrong information. There was an auction, but it had nothing to do with back taxes. That's all she knew.

A few minutes later she saw the house with its wide porch and cheery flower garden. An old, white truck was parked in front, and beside it, a blue compact car that had Tanner shaking his head and muttering. She didn't bother asking. She just looked around, until she saw the chestnut gelding and bay mare playing in the corral. The chestnut was a real beauty. Reminded her of Sir Galahad, the horse she'd been given for her twelfth birthday.

Tanner stopped the truck and parked right where they were between the house and barn, blocking everything. She just sighed. She'd hoped to stay in the truck and wait for him from a distance. Under the circumstances, it seemed almost rude to meet his family. After today, she doubted she'd ever see Tanner again.

She looked over at him, her heart catching at the sight of his familiar face…at the tiny mark where he'd cut himself shaving when she'd tickled him. Briefly she closed her eyes, then followed his gaze. A gray-haired man was coming out of the barn, wiping his hands with a rag.

"I'd better warn you, if you're planning on staying in the truck, Nana won't have it." Tanner was looking at her, confusion and regret darkening his hazel eyes.

She didn't imagine he cared that she was confused herself. He'd had a point about the watch. And it hurt to think she'd threatened him with a bogus lawsuit in the beginning. She'd felt guilty about it later, yet she hadn't set the record straight. So where did she get off being so angry with him?

The thing was, though, he knew how important it was for her to get him to Houston. She'd told him right after they'd made love. She'd laid herself bare, told him about the shaky relationship with her father, about how much she needed the job. It had never been just about the photo shoot. She needed this win. A lot was at stake, and Tanner should've known better than to take the controls from her.

"If it's any consolation, you won't be here long." Tanner had opened his door but was waiting for her answer. "I have to get you to the airstrip within two hours if you want to get to Houston this evening."

She nodded. Though she knew he wasn't wondering if she'd changed her mind about his offer. He had a childhood friend with a small plane who could fly her to Houston.

Tanner had promised he'd leave right after the auction and meet her there. She didn't really expect him to.

"What do you want me to do?" she asked. "Stay in the truck?"

His eyes met hers. He looked so tired, so defeated that something inside her softened. He moved his hand off the wheel, and she thought he would reach for her. But he only picked up his Stetson from the console. "Do what you want," he said. "I'll handle my grandmother."

The tightness in her chest swelled. He hadn't said it in a mean way, but she still wanted to cry. Just curl up into a little ball like a child and sob until she had no energy left to even think. Grateful she was wearing sunglasses, she watched Tanner embrace the tall, lean man from the barn. He had to be his grandfather, or Pop, as Tanner called him.

The front door slamming made her turn her head. An older blonde woman came hurrying off the porch and went straight to Tanner. He caught her in his arms and lifted her off the ground.

Then he set her on her feet and frowned at both of them. She couldn't hear what he said.

"Alexis?" The deep voice startled her, and she turned to see a man peering at her through the driver's open window.

She recognized the hazel eyes and slightly crooked smile. Although he had lighter hair, he resembled Tanner. "You must be Doug."

He nodded. "Warm day. How about coming inside?"

Hesitating, she swung a glance toward Tanner. He and his grandparents were walking toward the truck. Right away she saw where he got his stubbornness. Grandma had the same determined expression Lexy had seen on Tanner's face many times.

Wanting to avoid a scene, she went for the door handle. Tanner beat her to it. "You okay with coming inside?" he asked in a low voice, and when she nodded, he helped her step out of the cab.

She sent his grandparents a brief smile, praying this didn't get messy. She was an outsider and they had some serious talking to do. The horses, she thought, glancing toward the corral. She'd love to go see them.

"Relax," Tanner whispered, letting go of her arm. "This won't be as bad as you think."

"I'm Elizabeth Hill, the boys' grandmother," the trim woman said as they all headed to the porch. She had a friendly smile. "And this is Hank, their grandpa."

He nodded at her, and exchanged a small grin with Tanner.

"Yes, I'm aware I jumped the gun," Mrs. Hill said with a sigh, climbing the porch stairs after her husband. "But I'm still very upset about all this auction business. I told your grandpa we should've explained to you boys what we were doing."

"This is Alexis," Tanner said, waiting for Lexy to take the steps ahead of him.

"Of course, Doug told us you were coming. I have some lemonade to offer you, or water, but nothing else. We've been packing. But come in." Her face was flushed and it was clear she truly was upset. Tanner's boot only made it to the second step when his grandmother took his face in her hands. "How could you have ever thought you'd failed us? It breaks my heart. You're the best grandson anyone could ask for."

Doug noisily cleared his throat. Lexy felt for him, and quickly slid him a glance over her shoulder.

He was grinning.

"Oh, you, too, Douglas, you know that." Mrs. Hill hadn't released Tanner.

"Can we go inside before they all die of thirst?" It was

the first Mr. Hill had spoken. His voice was a bit gruff, but he had a kind, weathered face.

"Yes, yes, come in." Mrs. Hill moved first and held open the screen door.

Tanner gestured for Lexy to go inside, then waited for his brother to climb the porch steps. "Dammit, Doug, I told you not to cut your vacation short."

"Hell, I stopped listening to you when I was fourteen."

"Boys. Language. Please." Sighing, Mrs. Hill let go of the screen door. "Do you have brothers, Alexis?"

"Um, yes, one." Lexy pictured Harrison dressed in his custom-tailored suit, looking quite the Harvard man. Even as a child he'd been on the reserved side.

"Well, Hank and I had a girl…the boys' mother." She lifted a hand to her mouth as if to impart a secret. "Bless her heart, she was much easier than those two hellions."

Lexy couldn't help smiling. They entered the kitchen, and behind them Doug asked if his grandmother was telling tales about them. Lexy let the chatter go on around her as she took in the well-lit, airy kitchen. The Formica counters were mostly clear, everything packed away. She imagined there'd been a table sitting in the middle of the hardwood floor, before the furniture had been moved out. Something sturdy and old, maybe oak or cherry, perhaps passed down from earlier generations.

Mrs. Hill asked Doug to bring in two folding chairs then apologized to Lexy for serving lemonade in paper cups. The four of them chatted as if she weren't there, or more accurately, as if she'd been part of the family for years. Tanner didn't speak as much as the other three. Mostly he listened and watched her.

She tried to avoid eye contact with him. It was crazy how relieved she felt once she heard the real reason for the auction. The whole thing was a cooperative effort among several aging ranchers who wanted a little money to retire on and pass down. Cashing in had nothing to do with faltering mortgages or unpaid taxes, and more to do with love and respect for the next generation. The spreads were small, unable to compete with the larger ranches. By banding together they hoped to attract a bigger buyer and a better price. These people didn't want to burden their children and grandchildren, or hold them back from migrating to cities. They were looking out for their families.

Exhaustion combined with a mess of emotions over Tanner made it hard to sit still. Even worse, Lexy felt like one wrong word and she'd burst into tears. She looked up and found Tanner watching her shred the rim of her cup. He'd been so quiet, it bothered her. He should be happy, enjoying this time with the people who loved him, but he couldn't because of her.

He slid off his perch on the counter. "I have to get Lexy to the airstrip. I've got someone flying her to Houston."

"Oh, no, we've just met you." Mrs. Hill seemed genuinely disappointed. "I thought you were both staying. Not here, of course, we have no beds, but there's a nice motel—"

"Sorry, Nana. Lexy's on the clock. She's got business in Houston. I'll be joining her there tomorrow."

Lexy hated that her gaze shot to his. She wasn't sure what she expected to find there. He'd said all along he'd make it to the photo shoot. So now that he didn't have to go to the auction, why not drive with her? If they left now, they could stop someplace for the night…

Her body responded as if he'd touched her. She immediately stood. "So nice meeting all of you, Doug, Mr. and Mrs. Hill, and thank you for the lemonade," she said, unsure what to do with the cup.

Tanner took it from her nervous hands.

"Oh, heavens, call us Elizabeth and Hank. Although I wouldn't blame you one bit if you didn't want to speak to us again. Dragging all of you down here for nothing."

Hank slid an arm around his wife. "Who's flying her? Potter?" he asked, and Tanner nodded. "Good man. He'll get you to Houston in one piece."

Everyone walked them to the door, though Doug hung back, looking troubled. She wouldn't have been surprised if he asked to go for the ride, but she navigated the porch steps while silently praying he wouldn't.

Turned out it didn't matter. The ride to the airstrip was brief and mostly silent, though long enough that she had time to think about how she'd almost told Tanner she loved him. How foolish could she be? What did she know about love? Her parents' relationship wasn't exactly filled with sunshine and hearts, yet they weren't a bad match. Maybe love and marriage meant making the best deal possible and living with it.

Her phone buzzed. She sighed when she saw it was Harrison, and let it go to voice mail. What a bastard. Actually, she was shocked he'd been willing to call and hadn't texted her, instead. Perhaps he had more bad news to deliver, like she'd completely missed the photo shoot.

Tanner glanced over but didn't ask.

"I'm so sorry, Lexy," he said as soon as the airstrip came into view. "For all of this. I can't be mad at my grandparents—"

"Of course not." She resisted the urge to touch his arm. "They're nice people."

"Yeah, they are." He pulled up next to a building smaller than Betsy. "For their sake I won't strangle Archie Crawford, the neighbor who called. He is ninety, so…" Tanner shrugged.

It hurt that he let the engine run, but then she saw a short, stocky man signal to him. Tanner nodded and looked past the man toward the small plane. "I hate seeing you go up in that sucker."

Lexy smiled. "I'm safer in that plane than this truck."

His brows drew together in a frown. He'd taken it wrong. She didn't bother pointing out she'd meant statistically speaking. She hated the awkwardness between them.

"Ah, before I forget." He leaned sideways to dig into his jeans' pocket. "I'll take care of Potter's fee, but here's some cash for when you arrive."

"No, it's okay." She tried to pull her hand away but he caught her wrist and shoved a wad of bills at her.

"Let's not argue about this." His hand lingered on her wrist as he searched her face. "How about I put it on your tab?"

She smiled, nodded, turned away. The pilot was signaling again. She heard the driver's door open.

Tanner got out, grabbed her bag from the back and came around to her side. "I'll see you in Houston."

"Okay," she said, not believing it. Still, a part of her had hope or else she would just ask why he wouldn't leave now. "Look, I have something to tell you." She hoped she was doing the right thing. Yes, she was. No more secrets left between them. "Your father threw the game, that last hand. He folded but he had aces. I saw his cards."

"No. No way." Tanner's stricken expression chilled her. "You're telling me this now?"

"We gotta go, ma'am."

She turned to the pilot, then back to Tanner.

"Go," he said, and handed her the bag.

She hesitated. "I'll see you in Houston?"

"Be safe," he murmured absently, and got in his truck.

THE AUCTION HAD taken a total of ten minutes. Someone grumbled about setting up the table and chairs taking longer than the main event.

"I still can't believe the old man threw the game." Doug shook his head. "Hell, I can't believe what *you* just did."

Tanner signed the last of the paperwork his brother had

reviewed for him. "Does that change how you feel about him?"

"I honestly don't know."

"Same here." Tanner had been angry when Lexy had first told him about J.D. for two reasons. It upset Tanner's sense of fairness. And she should've told him on the spot.

But in the end, it had been the old man's decision to fold or take the pot. Yeah, Tanner had broken his father's lucky streak for nothing, but maybe J.D. could sleep better now. As for Lexy, it couldn't have been easy deciding what to do with the information. He understood that quandary all too well. Ultimately, she did what she thought was right, just like when she'd offered her watch. He knew she cared about him. He just wasn't sure how much.

They'd both been prideful and foolish, made choices they regretted, no matter that they'd sprung from good intentions.

Doug had done the same thing when he'd had Tanner take the Sundowner deal. That should've been Tanner's call. But he still loved his brother.

And dammit, he loved Lexy, too.

"You having buyer's remorse yet?" Doug asked as they walked out of the recreation building. "Not much fishing around here."

Tanner smiled, staring at the horizon. The morning sun had just risen above a thicket of mesquite. "Can you see me sitting around waiting for a damn nibble?"

"No." Doug laughed. "But you've stuck to that story for three years."

"I guess I figured Pop and Nana would live here forever. Mom grew up here. So did we, really. Thinking someone else would own the place got to me." Every pleasant memory he had was tied to his grandparents and the ranch, horses and rodeoing. When it had come down to the wire, he couldn't see himself doing anything else. He slid on his sunglasses and eyed Doug. "Call me old and sentimental, I don't care."

Doug shook his head. "Nope. I had that twinge, too," he said, a fist to his chest. "Right here. Only thing worries me is that you've made a big decision that ties you up here. You're in love with that woman, and I think she feels the same way."

Tanner's heart lurched. They hadn't talked about Lexy much. "If it's meant to be, Oklahoma City is less than a day's drive."

"Hey, you didn't tell me to screw off. You have changed."

He smiled. "It happens." Sometime last night he'd realized he'd been looking so hard at what he hadn't done right that he'd failed to give his future its proper due. Who cared if he quit rodeoing on a downslide? If he lost in the arena, it didn't make him a loser in life. That was his father's thinking, not his. Pride and poor choices had already kicked one Tanner male in the teeth.

He adjusted his hat and pulled out his keys. "Well, better get going."

"You gonna make it to Houston in time?"

"Damn straight. I gave Lexy my word."

THE HOTEL THE company had booked for everyone was first class, her room divine, boasting a mattress made in heaven. Lexy hadn't slept in a bed like that in ages. Too bad she'd gotten so little sleep last night.

Despite the rumbling in her stomach, she wasn't hungry. As she walked past the lobby, not even the smell of waffles and bacon coming from the restaurant tempted her. The photo shoot would begin in two hours. Tanner hadn't shown up. No surprise there, so that wasn't what had her tied in knots.

She knew for sure Harrison had sabotaged her by waiting until the last moment to give her an update. And if that wasn't hurtful enough, their father would be arriving soon to gloat over the damage he'd done to his children. Oh, he was pretending interest in the calendar. That was crap. He didn't sully his hands with that sort of thing.

He'd done a spectacular job with the company. Profits had soared under his leadership and the extended family members were all fat and happy. No one would argue Marshall Worthington had keen instincts and was a great CEO. As a father and head of his own family, he was an abysmal failure. She couldn't help wondering if he was proud of turning his two children against each other. But she didn't hate Harrison. She only hated what he'd done.

In a way she felt bad for him. He'd spent his life pedaling too fast, trying so hard to please, that he had no clarity. Even with all her debts, she wouldn't change anything.

Across the lobby the man himself walked out of the elevator. Harrison had been standing tête-à-tête with Karina, but quickly stepped away from her. Lexy thought of Tanner and how he would race through hell to help his family. Doug had cut short the only vacation he'd ever had. Even J.D. had come through in the end. Her own screwed-up family wouldn't cross the street for her. Or apparently, each other.

Her father spotted her and lifted a hand to get her attention. She knew the moment he noticed her suit was the same one she'd worn to his office last week, and she smiled.

"I heard you found your man," he said, adjusting his tie, then his gold cuff links.

"My…" She tensed, looking into her father's stern face, wondering how he'd found out about Tanner. Oh, for God's sake, now she understood.

"Yes, I did," she murmured, wondering was she really that far gone? Beyond hope? No, after a long night of soul searching she wouldn't change her mind about what she needed to do. Tanner was a little old-fashioned, and if she begged hard enough, and if he was willing to give her another chance, he'd probably make decisions for her again. But never out of malice, only from the best of intentions. She couldn't say the same for her own manipulative father. "Why are you here?"

Her brother had walked over to join them. At her abruptness, both men looked at her as if she'd lost her mind.

"Harrison, aren't you wondering why Dad would come to a photo shoot for a line of products he doesn't want?"

"What do you mean?" Harrison looked worried. "He approves."

"Come on. You don't believe that. You're too smart."

"Alexis, what's gotten into you?" Her father's icy glare raked her face, then drifted behind her.

Harrison was looking, as well, so she had to turn around.

"Tanner?" Her heart swelled at the sight of him in brand-new jeans with a crease, starched white shirt and a new brown Stetson. "God, Tanner." She headed toward him, blinking fast, trying to hold back tears. "You came."

He seemed pale. "I tell you what…" As if he just remembered, he yanked his hat off. "No way that puddle jumper is safer than my truck."

"Oh. No." She put a hand to her mouth. "You didn't."

"I promised you I'd be here."

"Your timing is perfect." She looked into his dark, hazel eyes. "It couldn't be more perfect. I know you might still be mad, and I hope…" She swallowed. "Will you kiss me?"

"Now?" His gaze went toward her father and Harrison.

"Yes."

"Um…"

"They're watching. I know." She moved closer and put her hands on his chest. "The hell with them. All I care about is you, and whether you'll give me another chance."

Tanner's slow smile made her melt. "I was gonna ask you the same thing. Right after the photo shoot."

"Nope. No photo shoot. They can't have you." Lexy slid her arms around him. "I have a great bed upstairs."

"I want to tell you something first. I went to the auction. Bought everything. A total of 450 acres." He smiled as her mouth opened in surprise. "When I talked to Matt Gunderson the other night, I realized I was jealous. Not that he was retiring at the top of his game, but because he seemed happy and settled and focused. I called him. He's gonna help me look into whether it's feasible for me to raise rodeo stock."

"So you'll be living at your grandparents' ranch?"

"I haven't figured out the details. I have to put quite a bit of money into the place. And that's another thing—"

"Don't even mention poker."

Tanner grinned. "I so much as think about betting more than ten bucks and you have my permission to take away my credit card and wallet."

"Okay, don't think I won't."

"Alexis!" It was her father. Tanner looked over at him. Lexy didn't.

"Daddy doesn't look happy. You might be out of a job."

"Oh, he can keep that."

He pulled her close. "Then you won't necessarily have to live in Oklahoma," he said, his heart beating faster as she shook her head. "I can't promise you a life of luxury, Lexy, but—"

"I don't need one. I mean, I want to pay my debts, but I do have a very fat trust fund available in a couple years."

"In the meantime, guess we'll have to rough it, living on my investments." He rubbed her back. "Doug says I still have a little over three million left. Probably doesn't sound like much to you but—"

Lexy laughed. "Shut up and kiss me."

Tanner touched her cheek and lowered his head. And made the whole world disappear.

Epilogue

One year later

"OH, DAMN." Lexy saw the smoke and shoved aside her laptop. "Harrison, I'll have to call you back," she said, swinging her feet to the floor.

"Come on, Lex. We need to finalize the quotes today."

"I'm burning down the house. I think that takes precedence." She disconnected, dropped her cell on the kitchen table, grabbed a potholder and opened the oven door.

Smoke poured out, setting off the smoke detector. Coughing, she backed up. It figured that Tanner and J.D. chose that moment to come through the kitchen door. Tanner swept off his hat and fanned the air, while his father shut off the shrieking alarm.

After the noise finally stopped and Lexy managed to transfer the dish from the oven to the stove, Tanner peered at the barely recognizable burnt casserole and asked, "Was that dinner?"

J.D. smiled and stared down at his boots.

"Yes," she said. "It's called Chicken Surprise." She sighed. "So, um, surprise. We're going out to eat."

"You could've just asked," Tanner said, grinning.

Lexy glanced at J.D., who wisely stayed quiet. "Your son never learns, does he?"

"I'm staying out of it," J.D. said and went to the fridge.

"Grab me a beer, too, Dad." Tanner blinked, looking shocked. He always called his father J.D.

His dad froze for a second, then opened the fridge door.

As far as Lexy knew, this was a first. In fact, they seemed to be having all kinds of firsts, lately. J.D. had been coming around regularly, helping Tanner with the livestock and installing the new irrigation system. She and Harrison had smoothed their differences and were starting a small company of their own. He still worked for The Worthington Group, but it was great to see him do something independently.

"Alexis." Tanner caught her hand. "Honey," he said, tugging her toward him. "After the new house is finished, before we move in, can we hire a housekeeper? One who can cook?"

"If you insist." She slid her arms around his waist and gave J.D. a private wink that made him chuckle.

Tanner leaned back to look at her. "Did you burn dinner on purpose?"

"No. I was busy," she said, glancing at her laptop. "I forgot to set the timer."

"I know you've got a lot on your plate." He kissed the tip of her nose. "And now that you're going to Oklahoma City every other week, I think we need to talk about our schedules."

"Not now, though, huh?" she said softly.

J.D. ambled out of the kitchen with his beer.

"Yeah, now, while J.D.'s here." Tanner brushed her hair back. "I want to get married."

Lexy blinked at him. They hadn't discussed marriage. They'd moved in to his grandparents' old house at the same time and hadn't been apart even for a night ever since.

"Okay." He cleared his throat, and tried to hide the hurt in his eyes. "If you don't like the idea, we can keep—"

"Yes." She squeezed him as hard as she could. "Yes, I want to marry you."

"You sure?"

"Positive." She hadn't meant to hesitate. Her own father had called to extend an olive branch earlier and had thrown her off track for most of the day. "Tonight, if you want."

Tanner smiled. "Don't you want a big, fancy wedding?"

"I want you," she whispered, gazing up into his handsome face. "That's all I want."

"I knew you were trouble, Alexis Worthington. The moment I laid eyes on you."

"Trouble?"

"Making me fall in love with you like you did." He kissed her. "I figured I was toast by the third day."

"Ah, you're so romantic," she said, grinning back. She touched the groove in his cheek. "I love you, Tanner."

He picked her up. "I love you so much sometimes it hurts."

"No, we'll never let love hurt." She shook her head. "Never."

"You're right. Never," he murmured and kissed her breathless.

* * * * *

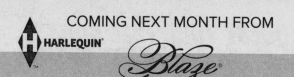

REQUEST YOUR FREE BOOKS!
2 FREE NOVELS PLUS 2 FREE GIFTS!

HARLEQUIN
Blaze®
red-hot reads!

YES! Please send me 2 FREE Harlequin® Blaze™ novels and my 2 FREE gifts (gifts are worth about $10). After receiving them, if I don't wish to receive any more books, I can return the shipping statement marked "cancel." If I don't cancel, I will receive 4 brand-new novels every month and be billed just $4.74 per book in the U.S. or $4.96 per book in Canada. That's a savings of at least 14% off the cover price. It's quite a bargain. Shipping and handling is just 50¢ per book in the U.S. and 75¢ per book in Canada.* I understand that accepting the 2 free books and gifts places me under no obligation to buy anything. I can always return a shipment and cancel at any time. Even if I never buy another book, the two free books and gifts are mine to keep forever.

150/350 HDN F4WC

Name	(PLEASE PRINT)	
Address		Apt. #
City	State/Prov.	Zip/Postal Code

Signature (if under 18, a parent or guardian must sign)

Mail to the **Harlequin® Reader Service:**
IN U.S.A.: P.O. Box 1867, Buffalo, NY 14240-1867
IN CANADA: P.O. Box 609, Fort Erie, Ontario L2A 5X3

Want to try two free books from another line?
Call 1-800-873-8635 or visit www.ReaderService.com.

* Terms and prices subject to change without notice. Prices do not include applicable taxes. Sales tax applicable in N.Y. Canadian residents will be charged applicable taxes. Offer not valid in Quebec. This offer is limited to one order per household. Not valid for current subscribers to Harlequin Blaze books. All orders subject to credit approval. Credit or debit balances in a customer's account(s) may be offset by any other outstanding balance owed by or to the customer. Please allow 4 to 6 weeks for delivery. Offer available while quantities last.

Your Privacy—The Harlequin® Reader Service is committed to protecting your privacy. Our Privacy Policy is available online at www.ReaderService.com or upon request from the Harlequin Reader Service.

We make a portion of our mailing list available to reputable third parties that offer products we believe may interest you. If you prefer that we not exchange your name with third parties, or if you wish to clarify or modify your communication preferences, please visit us at www.ReaderService.com/consumerchoice or write to us at Harlequin Reader Service Preference Service, P.O. Box 9062, Buffalo, NY 14269. Include your complete name and address.

HB13R2

Kate Hoffmann starts a new chapter in her
beloved miniseries with the New Zealand
Quinns—Rogan, Ryan and the namesake of the
April 2014 release

The Mighty
Quinns: Malcolm

Mal is the protector of his family, and right now
they need protection from nosy reporters.
Like Amy Engalls. She wants a story...unless he
can give her something better....

Amy could barely catch her breath. It was as if she was tumbling
down a mountainside and she couldn't gain a foothold. But
now that she'd gained momentum, she didn't want to stop.

Mal was the kind of guy she could only dream about
having—handsome, charming, fearless. And now, she'd been
handed the chance to be with him, to experience something
she might never find in her life again. Sure, she'd had lovers in
the past, but they'd never made her feel wild and uninhibited.
Just once, she wanted to be with a man who could make her
heart pound and her body ache.

Just a week ago, she'd been curled up on her sofa in her
Brooklyn flat, eating a pint of cherry chocolate-chip ice cream

and watching romantic comedies. That had been her life, waiting for Mr. Right. Well, it was time to stop waiting. She'd found Mr. Right Now here on the beach in New Zealand.

This wouldn't be about love or even affection. It would be about pure, unadulterated passion. This would be the adventure she'd never been brave enough to take. She wasn't about to pass this opportunity by. If she couldn't leave New Zealand with a story, then she'd leave with a damn good memory.

At the bedroom door, Mal stopped. He grabbed her hands and pinned them above her head, searching her gaze. "Are you sure this is what you want?" he murmured, pressing his hips against hers.

The quilt fell away, leaving Amy dressed only in her underwear. She could feel his desire beneath the faded fabric of his jeans—he was already completely aroused. Amy wanted to touch him there, to smooth her fingers over the hard ridge of his erection. She could be bold, too. "Yes," she said, pushing back with her body.

He kissed her again, his lips and tongue demanding a response. She did her best to match his intensity, and when he groaned, Amy knew that *she* was exactly what he wanted.

Pick up THE MIGHTY QUINNS: MALCOLM
by Kate Hoffmann, available March 18
wherever you buy Harlequin® Blaze® books.